Daddy Dom 2 in 1 novel collection

Say, Yes Daddy + Daddy's Naughty Baby

A DDLG and ABDL collection of kinky

BDSM age play stories

By Tina Moore

Table of Contents

Say, Yes Daddy

An ABDL age play romance about a
handsome Daddy Dom who introduces
his sweet and innocent baby girl to the
kinky lifestyle of DDLG

By Tina Moore

Chapter 1

Thank God it's Friday, Harvey thought as he watched the blonde with the thick ass stretch in front of him. She had been unknowingly teasing him for the last hour, and as her training session came to an end, all Harvey could do was keep his breathing constant as he fought the urge to rip her yoga pants off and bury his aching cock inside of her. *I'd cream-pie this bitch in every hole*, he thought, smiling to himself as he watched her bounce on her toes, her tits jiggling out of her sports bra as she stood, turning to face him.

"Well that's that good session, you worked hard today," Harvey said, wanting to get out of their as fast as he could. The blonde had been getting private training for the last month, and in that time she had done nothing but teased his cock. She had hardly even lost a pound, not that she needed too. She was a fitness model just wanting to maintain her shape in the off-season.

"Thanks, Harvey, see you next week," she said sweetly before walking off, apparently unaware of what he wanted to do to her. Harvey gave a sideward smile as he turned to go to his office. He had set up a private gym at the back of his property, wanting to work for himself after years of working in various gyms around the city. Harvey walked into his office, the air-con hitting him straight away and went to the cage Willow was laying in.

"Get out, I have a job for you," he said, grabbing her by the back of her head and dragging her out. The girl moaned as the vibrator he had stuffed inside of her an hour earlier moved as she crawled on her hands and knees to him. He sat down in his office chair and smiled as her white diapered bottom tried to grind down on the toy he knew was making her cunt leak cum. Harvey placed a hand in his pants and pulled out his hard bulging cock before roughly forcing it into

Willow's mouth, her eyes growing wide as his pre-cum ran down the back of her throat.

Willow had been living with Harvey for the last two months, and he had enjoyed keeping her as his fuck doll while he worked, making her be his cum whore in-between clients.

"That's it slut, suck Daddy's big cock. You love that don't you little girl; you love the way Daddy fucks your pretty little mouth. Swallow bitch," Harvey said, taking both of her hands and pinning them behind her back, making her fall back on her heels. Laying on the floor, Harvey sat on her face and watched as the tears began to roll down her face as he dumped his load down her throat, cum spilling out the sides of her mouth.

"Such a pretty little slut," he said, getting off her and walking into the shower. Leaving Willow laying on the floor in the middle of the office alone, his cum still dripping from her lips.

Millie shut her computer down and cracked her neck; it had been a long, hard week. Between her boss's insatiable desire to make her life a living hell and the long-term clients that she lost that week, Millie knew she needed a drink. *6:30*, she thought, looking out the window and breathing in deeply. In the five years, she had worked for the firm; she had never gone home before 6:30. The office was quiet, just the sound of the cleaners starting their shift and Millie wondered what she was doing with her life. Deciding to drop into a bar on her way home to her empty apartment, Millie stood, straightened her A-line pencil skirt and began making her way out of the building.

She passed about four blocks until she found the type of bar she felt comfortable going to. It was quiet, with only a few people sitting inside and most of the lounges free. She walked to the far side of the bar and sat down. From here, she could see who was coming in through the door and sighed as she sipped her drink. Millie took out her phone and began looking through the dating app she had downloaded earlier that week. Disappointed that the men she had matched with were only interested in fucking, she deleted the app and got up, knocking into someone and getting beer over her crisp white blouse.

"Oh I'm so sorry," Millie began gushing as she looked desperately for a napkin. Harvey smiled kindly and took her hand in his, stopping her and causing her to look up at him for the first time. She took in his tall stature, broad shoulders and thick head of hair that was slicked back to one side, his fade-away crisp on the other. Millie held her breath as she saw his dark denim jeans and well-fitting chambray shirt and bit her bottom lip.

"It's ok, I think you might need this more than me anyway," Harvey said, smiling a charmingly wicked smile. Mille smiled meekly, *God his voice is smooth*, she thought accepting the napkin Harvey offered her. Harvey gestured for Millie to sit back down and he re-ordered his beer, pausing to see what she wanted.

"Oh no it's alright," Millie said not wanting to inconvenience Harvey.

"Please?" Harvey said cheekily causing

Millie to laugh.

"I'll have what you're having," Millie replied as Harvey placed his hand on the back of her chair. They waited in silence while the bar attender poured the two beers and Millie wondered how she had been so lucky to have such a handsome man turn up to a bar like this one. *Surely he was on his way to a party or something and just came in here for a quiet drink; he's probably just drinking with me because he feels sorry for me*, she thought before thanking the bar attender. Harvey looked over his beer glass at Millie while he drank, winking at her before he put the glass down.

"So, do you always drink by yourself?" He asked, making Millie blush. *Oh, she's cute*, Harvey thought, placing his hand on her thigh, squeezing slightly. Millie was surprised how bold he was being, and it made her cunt ache to be touched instantly.

"Well, no, usually I wouldn't be here at all, but it's Friday, and you know, I just thought maybe I could use a drink," Millie said, stumbling on her words. Harvey just smiled back at her, kindly. *I wonder how this goes down*; he thought as he finished his beer.

"Look, you are so sweet, how about I take you out of this shit-hole, and we go somewhere a little nicer?" He suggested making Millie feel uneasy. She shifted in her seat and tucked her hair behind her ear before looking up at him.

"I don't do that sort of thing," she said, finishing off her beer. Harvey nodded his head understandingly before writing his number down on a napkin.

"Then you'll need this, for when you change your mind," he said making Millie laugh. She watched as Harvey stood up, paid the bar attender and made his way to the door, realizing that she had never even introduced herself or knew his name. She quickly stood and raced after him, grabbing his arm and making him turn around, surprised to be touched so desperately.

"I never introduced myself, I'm Millie," she said, realizing that it was going to be a cold night and that her beer-soaked blouse was making her chest even colder. Harvey took his large brown leather jacket off and draped it over Millie's shoulders.

"Most people call me Harvey," he said, making Millie look confused.

"What do the other people call you?" Millie asked as Harvey pulled the front of the jacket closed on Millie, gently rubbing his thumbs over her hard nipples which were visible through her bra and blouse.

"Daddy," Harvey whispered as he bent down to kiss Millie's cheek before turning on his heel and walking around the corner.

Chapter 2

Harvey had been on her mind all night. Millie had gone home and practically ran to her computer, logging onto her favorite porn site and fucking her desperate cunt for hours. Harvey's jacket still on her shoulders and her arms hurting, she had called it a night by 1:15 in the morning and had fallen asleep in her chair.

Harvey had gone home too, but his night was vastly different from Millie's. He had used Willow like the fuck doll she was, stretching her ass and filling it with as much cum as it would take before diapering her and chaining her to his bed.

"Hi, is this Harvey?" Millie asked into her phone the next morning. She hadn't been able to fight the urge to call him. She needed to hear his smooth, sexy voice again.

"Yes, it is Miss Millie. How are you?" Harvey replied as calm as ever. Millie giggled hearing the way Harvey was speaking with her, and she involuntarily rubbed herself over her fluffy pajama shorts. Although it was the middle of winter, the heating in Millie's apartment made it feel like spring, and she enjoyed being able to wear her short shorts and tight white racer back singlet around the house.

"I was just ringing to see when I can return your jacket to you," Millie said, her voice going high.

"No, you're not. Your call has nothing to do with my jacket, tell me why you are calling," Harvey said, sounding slightly more severe. Millie swallowed hard as she felt her body betray her, and her panties get wet.

"I want to see you again," Millie said softly. Harvey leaned back; he had been sitting in bed, slapping Willow's open mouth with his cock until now. He got up and enjoyed that Willow had to stay in bed as he began to rub his hardening cock in front of her.

"When are you free?" Harvey said, trying to keep his breathing constant. Millie giggled.

"I'm free tonight?" She said, hoping that Harvey would agree. Harvey stroked his cock through his large hands, shaking it slightly and watched as Willow turned around obediently. Harvey climbed back up into bed and placed Willow's panties in her mouth before he slipped the tip of his cock into her soft, pink pussy.

"Tonight would be perfect. Let's meet at our bar, and we can go from there. Say 7?" Harvey said, reaching around and rubbing Willow's clit, making her shake her hips on him.

"7 would be perfect, see you then," Millie said making Harvey smile and end the call as he plunged into Willow's ready cunt.

"Daddy's got a date tonight baby girl, do you know what that means?" Harvey said, throwing the phone onto the bed and placing both his hands on Willow's motherly hips. He pumped aggressively in and out of her making her moan and dip her head in submission as he nailed her.

"No? Ok, let Daddy tell you then. It means that Uncle Ben is going to come over and take care of you. And I'm going to leave you dirty and used so that if he wants you, he'll have to fuck you over the top of Daddy's cum, so you know that I'm always there. Would you like that baby girl? My little whore," Harvey said, feeling Willow's juices break inside of her and gush out around his cock.

"Yeah, I thought so," Harvey laughed, slapping her ass dismissingly before he pulled out of her and came on her back.

"Come here, jam jams time," Harvey said unchaining Willow and pulling up her purple onesie over her used body. Harvey held her in his arms.

"Will you be a good girl for Daddy and let Uncle Ben play with you the way he wants baby girl?" Harvey asked Willow, who was smiling widely and nodding her head. Willow liked to be taken a lot rougher than Harvey would have usually wanted to give, but she had been thrown out of her last Daddy's house after she broke a rule he had. Harvey had thought it was stupid of him to not just punish her for it, throwing her out seemed a bit extreme and such a waste. She had contacted Harvey asking if she could stay a few nights while she sorted out getting a new apartment, but things had moved fast. With Harvey fucking her on the first night and he had let her stay with the knowledge that their relationship was not ever going to be long-lasting. Willow had understood that Harvey didn't want a girl like her who wanted to be used so viciously and share, but she still enjoyed having him for as long as she had.

Willow nodded her head and gasped as Harvey pulled her panties out of her mouth.

"Yes, Daddy," she replied, receiving a gentle slap on her face as Harvey got up to get ready for the day.

"Hi," Millie said, enjoying how Harvey looked at her the minute their eyes met. She had taken her time getting ready tonight, deciding on a soft pink dress with white stockings and pink heels. Her blonde hair was down, and her blue eyes sparkled as the lights of the bar reflected in them. Harvey was not the only impressed one, as the eyes of the other men in the dive of a bar continued to steal long, lustful stares at the 24-year-old.

"Howdy," Harvey replied, kissing her on the top of her head and gesturing to the bar attender to pour two beers. Millie couldn't help herself and brought her arms up to hug Harvey's waist, enjoying the feel of his big belt buckle pressing against her tummy.

"How have you been sweetie?" Harvey said, stroking her hair before sitting down. He took off his dark grey felt coat and began to roll up the sleeves of his oxford cotton button down, showing off his muscular forearms. Millie hadn't realized she had been staring until he cleared his throat and tilted his head slightly.

"Oh I've been fine, um, here," Millie said, snapping herself back into reality and passing

Harvey his jacket. He smiled, accepting it again and hung it over the back of the bar stool. She nervously began to tear at the cuticles of her manicured hands, making her nail slightly bleed.

"Baby girl, you hurt yourself," Harvey involuntarily said, frowning and reaching into his jeans pocket, to Millie's surprise, pulling out a plaster.

"Here," Harvey said lovingly, catching Millie off guard. She watched in awe as Harvey gently took her hand in his and placed the plaster over her finger.

"There, all better, no more of that," he said, making her blush and pull away from him, looking down at the princess plaster he had just put over her finger.

"Great, no I look like I'm a little girl," Millie laughed, holding up her finger to show him. Harvey just smiled a knowing smile and leaned back in his stool, picked up his beer, and took a sip.

"Aren't you?" He said smirking when Millie raised an eyebrow at him.

"Um, no!" She exclaimed, looking herself up and down. Harvey just placed his hand on her cheek and stroked it with his thumb.

"Well, that's not what I see, baby girl," he replied before gesturing that they should leave the bar.

"Where do you want to go?" Millie said, standing up and reaching for her coat that Harvey already had in his hands.

"Turn around," he said kindly making Millie roll her eyes dramatically before following his instructions. Harvey wasn't like the guys she had had before. They had all been jerks who treated her like she was just something to brag about. But Harvey was handsome and gentle and made her feel like she could never be hurt again. She cursed herself for feeling so obsessed with him when it was only the first time they were spending any time together.

"Let's go, baby," Harvey said, holding out his hand to her. She playful pushed it away before walking confidently out of the bar in front of him.

He smiled at his feet and walked out after her, quickly grabbing her by her upper arm and pulling her back to him.

"Hold Daddy's hand, baby girl," he said while his other hand snaked its way around her waist. Millie swallowed hard and bit the side of her bottom lip as she felt Harvey's hard cock press into the back of her dress. She stayed there, letting him softly grope at her before he turned her around and looked at her deep in her eyes.

"Just let me know if you want to stop, ok?" Harvey said, bending down and kissing the tip of her nose. Millie nodded her head and wrapped both her arms around his large arm as they waited for a taxi.

Harvey took Millie to a family owned Mexican restaurant down a small side alley, and Millie had been blown away that he would know somewhere so quaint and magical. They talked about art and what their dreams where both laughing that they thought working a 9-5 was a ridiculous waste of life and Millie reached for Harvey's hand as they walked back out onto the street.

"Harvey, I've had a charming time," Millie said. Harvey looked down to see she was smiling up at him, her big blue eyes catching the moonlight.

"I'm glad you have little one. Do you have space in there for one more thing?" Harvey said, walking them over to a park bench and sitting her on his lap. Millie was surprised how relaxed she was with him as she rested her head on his broad chest and nodded sleepily up at him.

"Good," Harvey said, unbuckling his belt and subtly reaching under Millie's dress. She gasped as she felt his hand in her stockings, pressing on her slit and holding her firmer when he found how wet she was. Millie could feel his cock getting hard again, bulging between her thighs and pushing into her.

"Can Daddy fill you up, baby girl?" Harvey said lifting Millie slightly and repositioning his thick cock, ready to bury it up his sweet date.

Millie just nodded as Harvey gently reached both hands under her dress and pulled her stockings down, before lifting her and placing her down onto his erect shaft, making her take it all at once as he lowered her back onto him. Millie squirmed at the size of the cock filling her, unsure if it was too big for her to take and waited for her muscles to relax around the monster that had invaded her.

"Daddy, I," was all Millie could say before Harvey covered her mouth with his hand and wrapped his other one around her waist.

"You said you still had room, little one," he teased, keeping still as not to hurt her. He felt Millie clench her cunt around his cock, and he placed his hands on both sides of her ass, lifting her again before letting her drop down from a couple of inches from his lap.

"Good thing no one is around to hear your little moans, baby girl," Harvey laughed as he repeated his actions, forcing Millie to take him harder and harder. Millie just placed her hands on his knees, bending forward and feeling him deeper inside of her.

"I can't," Millie said, struggling to get down from Harvey's lap, wanting his huge cock out of her. He helped her, lifting her and off him and placing her gently on her shaking legs, quickly catching her as her legs gave way underneath her. Putting his still hard cock back in his pants, Harvey held Millie in his arms, wrapping his opened coat around her as her breathing returned to normal.

"Are you alright, baby girl? Teddy is quite greedy, but he likes filling up your pretty princess parts. Next time maybe he'll fill you up with his Teddy cream too," Harvey said, stroking his cock over his jeans. Millie didn't know what came over her, but she began to suck her thumb as he cuddled her, watching him stroke down his hard erection.

"Teddy?" She softly asked Harvey, who just nodded. He took her hand and placed it over the pole that was kept down by his tight jeans making her stroke it for him.

"Teddy is clever, he can make you scream

and giggle at the same time," Harvey replied, making Millie giggle before going back to sucking her thumb.

"Come on baby, let's get you home," he added, reaching under Millie's skirt and putting her panties and stockings back in place before taking her free hand and walking her back out onto the main road.

Chapter 3

"Willow, do you want milk with your coffee?" Harvey said three days later. He had known that he needed to cut her loose the minute he speared Millie with his cock. He found her willingness to be taken and used was so perfectly complimented by her sweet femininity that he couldn't imagine not having her in his life. Millie had messaged him daily, asking him all the questions a new date would. They had shared their childhood stories, how they had chosen their careers, and what they looked for in a partner. Millie had explained that she had never been with a guy who called himself Daddy and Harvey sent her a few internet links for her to read different articles about the DDlg kink. He was relieved that she had messaged back saying that she wasn't sure if she wanted all that the kink covered but that she liked what they had done so far.

"Yeah, of course, I do," Willow replied, looking over her laptop annoyed that he had asked. Harvey rolled his eyes and took the milk jug in one hand and the morning paper in the other. He sat down, deciding that today would be the day he let her go. He had contemplated how he should do it; he had no feelings for the woman but still didn't want just to throw her out, ending the relationship like her last one.

"Wills, it's that time," Harvey said, placing the paper on the table and pouring the milk into her coffee cup. Willow looked her green eyes up without moving her head.

"You look like a demon like that," Harvey smirked watching her face. She lifted her head and sipped her coffee.

"She's that good is she?" Willow teased getting up and kissing Harvey's cheek as she passed, going into the kitchen and taking down the cereal before walking back to the table.

"Yeah, she is," he replied flicking through

his phone looking at the photos Millie had just sent him. She was sitting on the floor, on her knees, her soft thighs open, light blue lace panties covering her creamy white pussy. The photo was cut off at her nipples, and he liked how innocent she was. Putting his phone away, Harvey looked back up at Willow who was busy typing on her keyboard.

"So, let's look for a place you can move into?" He suggested flicking through the paper to the real estate section.

"Already on it," Willow said, smiling, turning the laptop around and coming to sit on his lap. He knew what she was doing and reached around to rub her naked pussy.

"You're such a fucking slut Willow," he laughed, pushing his two fingers into her roughly making her bend forward and gasp as he pounded her knuckle deep.

"Thank you, Harvey," she breathlessly panted, aware that he was giving her what she wanted.

"It's ok sweetie, cum for me and then we

need to find you someone who will look after this little cunt the way you need it," Harvey said holding her down by her neck and pulling his fingers from her cumming pussy. He reached into his pants and pressed the tip of his cock into her ass, taking her by surprise.

"Take it, bitch, don't you dare fucking refuse me," Harvey growled slapping her ass and thighs until she relaxed and let him slide into her, stretching her as he gently jerked his cock inside her, his cum squirting into her. Pulling out, he went to the kitchen drawer and rolled on a condom.

"Get down here," he said snapping his fingers to the couch and taking Willow's wrist in his large hand and threw her down before getting on his knees and stabbing her wet pussy with his long thick cock fucking the air out of her lungs.

"Willow, it'll be alright," Harvey said as tears began to roll down her cheeks. He stood up, careful to keep his cock buried deep inside her and lifted her, holding her in his arms as she was fucked. He took her arms and held them behind her back as his other arm held her up, bouncing her up and down on his rod, forcing her to be fucked slightly beyond her limit. He knew that he was just over the line by her limp submission, her head resting on his shoulder, his chest wet with her tears.

"I've got you, you're ok," Harvey said lovingly. He kissed the top of her head before letting go of her arms and feeling them flying around his neck as he continued to force long strokes inside her, hitting her hilt and pushing into her. Feeling his cock push her tummy out. Her muscles destroyed.

"That's enough sweetie," he said, flicking cum onto the wooden floor as he lifted her off the pulsing cock that just fucked her to exhaustion. He lowered her onto the sofa and went into his bedroom, collecting a packet of wet wipes and her blanket. Walking back into the kitchen, he filled her sippy cup with warm milk and found her pink chew toy before he came back by her side and sat on the floor next to the sofa as he wiped down her dripping cunt. He took out a new wipe and wiped her face, kissing the tip of her nose and cupping her face in both his hands.

"No more little one," Harvey said, looking into Willow's wide eyes, her head nodding as Harvey began to tuck the blanket around her shivering body. He passed her the sippy cup and patted her tummy as she drank, her eyes closing and her smaller hands resting on top of his.

"What happened to you?" Harvey said, knowing that she was trying to fuck away some deeply, set in pain that someone had done to her.

"No Harvey," was all Willow replied, knowing that there was no way to explain the pain she was feeling, that she hadn't even let herself explore it to understand what it was that harmed her so powerfully. Harvey just nodded and stroked her forehead as she passed him back her empty milk cup and began chewing on the pink teething ring that she had successfully torn apart in one selection.

"I'll get you a new one before you go," Harvey said frowning at how damaged she had made her current one.

"I can do that myself, Harvey. I'm grateful to you, really, but it is ok, you don't have to care for me anymore," Willow said smiling a genuine smile, her hard eyes softening for a moment before turning cold again.

Millie had read up on the DDlg kink for days, getting turned on watching different porn videos and realizing that there was a whole new world that she hadn't ever considered exploring before. She wondered how Harvey had found it and had just short of 50 thousand questions she wanted to ask him. Delighted when he rang shortly after she had sent a slight cock tease of a photo, she picked up more quickly than she usually would have.

"Hi," Millie excitedly said down the phone, causing Harvey to laugh involuntarily.

"Hey sweetie, what are you up to?" Harvey said, sitting in the hammock outside on the back porch. From his position, he over-looked the downward slope, which leads to the pond. He had introduced ducks to the lake two years ago and watched as they swam around dipping their head under the water as Millie told him all the things she had done in the last three days.

"Wow, baby girl sounds like you've been busy! Of course, I can answer your questions, do you want to meet up somewhere a little more private so we can talk openly?" Harvey suggested, looking up at the white clouds that scattered across the sky.

"Sure, where are you thinking?" Millie asked. Harvey thought for a moment before placing his hand on his cock, playing with his balls as he spoke.

"Want to come over and see my house?" He asked, a cheeky grin spreading across his face. Millie laughed.

"You just want to play Harvey!" She accused, and Harvey gave a sideward smile.

"Now look, if I wanted to play, do you think

I wouldn't just take you when and where I wanted to? Didn't I spread your thighs and push Teddy deep inside you the minute I wanted to last time?" Harvey said, his cock hardening under his grey sweat pants as he spoke the words that made Millie gasp, her cunt aching instantly.

"Yeah, I guess you did," she replied, wondering where the conversation would go.

"And didn't I stop the minute you wanted to?" He added, smiling at himself as he felt like such a good guy for doing the only thing he should have.

"Yeah," Millie said cautiously.

"Well, I guess you can trust me then sweetheart can't you?" Harvey asked, remembering how tight Millie was, how his 8 inches almost didn't fit.

"I'll send you my address, let me know how long it takes you and when you are on your way little one, Daddy wants to make sure I've set up our afternoon tea spread in time," Harvey said as he slowly jerked off before hanging up the phone.

He got up out of the hammock and took his shirt off, letting it fall onto the grass and as he pulled his designer sweats down slightly as he jerked off in the privacy of his expansive back yard.

"Fuck this is good," Harvey moaned as he shot his load onto the grass, happy to be able to be so free. He laughed to himself as he put his cock back into his pants, enjoying the feeling of the soft material against his wet rod, bent down to pick up his white T-shirt and headed back inside to find that Willow had gone to his bedroom.

"I'm going to have company Willow, is there something you can do for tonight?" Harvey said, throwing his clothes into the wash basket and stepping into the shower.

"Will?" He asked when no reply came. Willow took her earphones from her ears and looked at him, confused.

"Huh?" She asked, walking into the bathroom and watched as Harvey washed his chiseled body. He ran his soapy hands over his rippled abs, his side tattoo moving as his muscles flex when he reached around his back.

"Have you got something to do tonight? I'm having a guest," Harvey said, repeating himself and letting the water run over his head before he shook his hair and leaned back against the shower wall.

"Oh, yeah, no trouble. I'll be gone all weekend if that's cool," Willow said, biting her lip as she watched Harvey run his fingers through his hair.

"Good," he said, turning around, dismissing her. Willow tightened her pussy as she turned and walked away, racking her brain as to what she could spend her weekend doing.

Chapter 4

"Well hello there precious," Harvey said, opening the door seeing Millie kneeling in front of him. She had obliviously dropped her handbag, the contents sprawled out over the front steps.

"Let me help you, little lady," he added, bending down and helping her pick up her things. Millie blushed and looked at him sheepishly before clearing her throat.

"Hi Daddy," she softly said, biting her lip, hoping that she was saying the right thing.

"Oh baby," Harvey said scooping Millie up with one arm and picking her bag up with the other as he carried her into his house. Millie gasped as she saw the country style house, the dark timber wooden floors, and cowhide in the living room, the big fireplace and smelt the vanilla and berry scented candles.

"Wow," was all Millie could say as she was caught off guard by Harvey's sophisticated and stylish home.

"I'm glad you like it," Harvey whispered in Millie's ear, gently lowering her to the floor, making sure she was settled on her feet before he let her go entirely.

"I'll just put your bag over here sweetie," Harvey said, placing her bag next to the sofa before taking her hand and leading her through the house to the back porch. He had set up fairy cakes and tea and coffee over the white linen table cloth on the whitewashed wooden table that overlooked the pond.

"Harvey," was all Millie could say becoming overwhelmed with the beauty of his home.

"No baby, I'm Daddy," Harvey tenderly said, pulling the chair out for Millie who absent-mindedly sat and nodded.

"Yes, Daddy," she answered as Harvey sat next to her and offered her coffee.

"Um no, may I have tea please?" Millie

asked, pulling herself away from the view and looking into Harvey's sparkling brown eyes. Harvey put the coffee jug down and placed his hand gently on Millie's cheek, pushing his thumb into her mouth, happy she didn't resist him.

"Say, please Daddy," Harvey prompted, enjoying having a new baby to teach.

"Please Daddy," Millie said around Harvey's thick thumb. He kept it in her mouth as he poured her the tea.

"When Daddy puts something in your mouth baby girl, I want you to suck it until I take it out, alright?" Harvey said, watching as Millie's lips form a pout around his thumb as she began to obey his instruction.

"Good girl baby Millie," Harvey said, feeling her tongue stroke him as she sucked.

"Clever girl. You're going to be a good girl for Daddy won't you," Harvey said as he reached out to grope Millie's massive breasts. He liked that she had a small frame and large fuck-able tits. *She's going to be perfect, her tits are so full and ripe, they*

are going to look so good bound, and cock fucked,
Harvey thought getting hard under the table.
Taking his thumb out of her mouth, he smiled
lovingly and placed a cake on her plate.

"So, what do you want to know?" Harvey
asked biting the wings off his cake and wiping the
cream that stayed on his bottom lip with his index
finger before sticking it in Millie's mouth, getting
aroused by how her full lips looked with his thick
finger stuffed in her little mouth.

"Oh, baby is a quick learner," Harvey said
excitedly as Millie sucked his finger deep into her
throat. Harvey waited longer than he needed to
before taking his finger from her lips.

"Like, do you like all this sort of stuff?"
Millie said, reaching for her phone and beginning
to flick through wanting to show him the photos
she had saved. Harvey took her photo and put it on
the other side of the table.

"Use your words little one," he said, making
Millie blush as she tried to form the words she had
never spoken in this context before.

"Like, diapers and stuff," she said, trying to hide her embarrassment. Harvey sat back and enjoyed her discomfort before handing her the phone again.

"Yes, I like dressing my partner in diapers and stuff," he teased using her words as he let her find the photos.

"Like this?" Millie asked, showing him the album she had created. He flicked through the photos of women in diapers and onesies, the ones with pacifiers in their mouths and Daddies who had stuff their cocks into the diaper covered pussies of their babies. He stopped on a photo of a woman in a pink dress, her pink diaper showing as she was bent over an older man's lap and spanked. Her legs were bound, and her arms were cuffed behind her back as a vibrator had been pushed into her pussy, and a dildo was used to gag her.

"Do you like the idea of this?" Harvey asked, raising an eyebrow at Millie, knowing that anything he said or did with her, would make her feel humiliated in lustful shame.

"Yes, Daddy," Millie softly said, biting her bottom lip. Harvey saw that she hadn't eaten her cake and he took a fork and broke off a piece for her, feeding her the mouthful as her eyes went wide as she opened her mouth.

"I think you are going to love being mine sweetheart. Daddy is going to treat you real good," Harvey said, kissing her lips, parting them with his tongue, tasting her vanilla bean frosting covered tongue. He moaned as he got up, knocking his chair backward as he kicked it away and lifted Millie into his arms. He took her chin in his hand, holding her mouth to his as he walked down to the hammock, all the while tasting her and feeling her grind into his waist. Harvey lay down on the hammock and placed Millie on top of him, feeling the weight of her heavy tits and hard nipples through her tight printed T-shirt. Harvey carefully grabbed a fistful of her hair, pulling her head backward slowly and looking into her eyes. Millie placed her hands on his chest, and he liked how it felt as she pushed against him and sat up, straddling his lap, her knees up like a little frog. Her short flowy skirt had fallen back, exposing her puffy pussy pressing hard against light pink cotton panties, the subtle line of her wetness making Harvey's fingers reach up to touch her.

"God you are so beautiful Millie," Harvey said, pulling her panties to the side and stroking her up and down her wet slit, feeling the small bud of her clit hot under his touch. He continued to stroke her as she began to grind against his fingers, resting both her hands on his chest, her tits being squeezed between her arms. She could feel him as she slowly dry humped his camel colored trousers enjoying his hardening bulge pushing into her ass, his fingers only adding to her frustration.

"Tell Daddy what you want, baby girl," Harvey said bucking his hips making Millie bounce on his fingers, being touched deeper than she had been prepared for, her gasp as he entered her without warning making her eyes go wide.

"Please fuck me, Daddy," Millie said

desperately, grinding down hard on Harvey's fingers as they began to slowly wiggle inside of her, his thumb flicking her clit in time with his slow onslaught. Millie moaned and closed her eyes as he edged her closer to orgasm. Harvey licked his lip before reaching into his pants and pulling out his erect cock, rubbing his full balls.

"Not yet, baby girl," he whispered, sitting up and taking his fingers from Millie who whimpered in frustration only adding to his arousal.

"What do I have to do to get fucked, Daddy?" Millie said involuntarily as she grabbed his cock and began jerking him off. Harvey laughed and took her hands away, making Millie confused as to why he was rejecting her touch.

"Those are some very big words young lady," Harvey teased, enjoying having Millie a hot mess ready to do whatever he asked.

"You haven't finished your cake yet sweetie, I can't have that little tummy of yours empty," Harvey said as he jerked himself off, rubbing his cock up and down Millie's slit.

"Then fill me with Teddy," Millie said, bending her head and licking his balls. Harvey pushed himself into her mouth, placing his hand on the back of her head and forcing both his cum filled balls into her mouth until she gagged. His pre-cum dripping onto Millie's cheek as she sucked his heavy sack.

"Suck Daddy like a good girl," Harvey said, pushing her head down and pushing his balls down her throat, moaning as he felt her gag around them.

"You surprise me, baby girl," Harvey said, slapping his rock hard cock against Millie's face. Millie could feel the fresh air of the afternoon turning into night as her ass wiggled in the air, spit dribbling from her lips and onto Harvey's trousers. Her skirt had fallen to rest on her back, her bubble butt jiggling much to Harvey's delight as he thrust into her mouth. Suddenly feeling her head being pulled back, Harvey wiped the saliva from her chin and turned her around, so she was facing away from him.

"Let's warm you up a little bit," Harvey said, pulling the side of Millie's panties up on the side of her ass and pushing his cock along her ass crack. He held her hips in his hands, licking his lips as he saw how she looked having his cock rubbing up and down her soft skin. Slapping Millie's hands away when she tried to reach for his cock, Harvey began trusting more feverishly against her skin, his wet balls slapping against the side of her ass as he came hard, his load dripping down into her ass crack, pooling at her ass-hole.

"Daddy made a mess, baby girl, let's see if I can tidy you up," Harvey said rubbing his oozing cock up and down her slit, covering her, claiming her cunt as his. He bent over her, reaching for her tits, pulling on them like he was milking her as his cock rested under her panties at the top of her ass.

"If anything is ever too much, you need to tell Daddy red ok, baby? I don't ever want to do something you don't like, that's not fun for me," Harvey said pulling on Millie's nipples and flicking them as the first stars began to flicker across the open sky.

"Yes, Daddy. What do I say if I want you to smash my cunt?" Millie asked feeling cheeky and hornier than she had ever in her life. Harvey laughed and placed both his hands on the back of Millie's panties and slowly pulled them down, moving her thighs together and pushing her head down.

"You say, please Daddy," Harvey said pushing his cock past Millie's soft, puffy pussy lips and straight into her cunt, her panties forcing her knees together and his thighs pinning her body down. Millie moaned and tried to buck her ass back but was only met with another powerful thrust of Harvey's hips, spearing her aching cunt but this time he kept it inside of her loving how her muscles tighten around his cock as it intruded into her most precious place.

"If you want, little girl, Daddy will make you his," Harvey said, placing his hands on her wrists and holding them down in front of her, stretching her arms forward.

"Please, Daddy," Millie moaned as though she was breathing for the first time. Harvey pulled out just to force himself inside her again, her legs beginning to shake. He fucked her balls deep, enjoying how his orgasm started to build in time with Millie's. Deciding that he wanted to surprise Millie with one more tease, Harvey got up and pulled out of her abruptly making her whine in frustration of her orgasm denial.

"Daddy doesn't care if you cum or not baby girl. Your pussy is for my enjoyment, not yours. If you cum, lucky you, but if you don't, don't complain to Daddy," Harvey said getting out of the hammock, his need to cum so intense it was almost painful.

"Yes, Daddy," Millie said as he repositioned her so that she was on all fours, facing the pond, her dripping pussy glistening in the moonlight as Harvey positioned himself behind her, pushing his cold, cum-covered cock back into her warm cunt. He grabbed her hips and buried himself deep inside her, pushing her hips away, making her swing on the hammock before coming back only for her pussy to be pierced by Harvey's pulsing shaft. Her pussy lips splitting as Millie's pussy gobbled up Harvey's cock with each swing back, her hilt being hit time after time.

"Stay like that, sweetie," Harvey said slapping Millie's ass lovingly as he saw her arms begin to shake as the hammock swung back, again forcing her pussy to take Harvey's cumming cock, being squirted with his cream each time he filled her. Her cunt quickly taking all of him, his balls full and soft against her ass as he held the hammock in place and pushed them into her. Holding the hammock in place with one hand, Harvey reached around and grabbed the front of Millie's throat as he began to pound her powerfully, feeling her cum squirt against his cock, feeling his cum mixing inside of her and spilling from her hole and down her thighs. Tightening his grip, he felt Millie gasp for air just as he pulled out his now limp cock. He pushed Millie down on the hammock as her breaths came in shallow gasps, and her pussy juices still pouring from her as she lay spent. The hammock swung gently in the night breeze as Harvey sat back on the grass, catching his breath. He heard Millie's breath return to normal and watched as she cautiously looked over the top of the hammock to stare at him.

"Are you ok, baby girl? Did Daddy hurt you at all?" Harvey said as Millie just shook her head, despite the tears that were being to fall from her eyes.

"Oh, baby, what is it?" Harvey said as he stood quickly, worried he had hurt her.

"I have never been fucked like that before," Millie said as he cupped her face in his hands. Harvey just smiled as he saw Millie work through her space, reaching into the hammock to pick her up and began to carry her back to the house.

"Daddy likes carrying you like a princess," Harvey said, placing Millie down on his bed. He gently rolled her panties the rest of the way down her legs, took off her skirt, T-shirt, and bra, getting a surprise when he saw her nipples where pierced.

"Naughty little girl!" Harvey exclaimed, marveling at how pink her nipples were. The piercing bars forcing her nipples to stay hard, the large buds looking like buttons Harvey knew he wanted to tease all over again. Millie saw the desire in his eyes.

"You can if you want Daddy," she said, her little voice surprising her as she heard it for the first time. It didn't escape Harvey either, and he took in her form. Her body was soft, the thin layer of untoned tummy over her abs jiggling when he placed his hand on her and patted her gently.

"You are such a good girl for Daddy, but I think you've had enough sweetie," Harvey said, making Millie smile and close her eyes, exhausted psychologically as well as physically. Harvey took his navy cable knit sweater off, his white T-shirt clinging to his bulk mass. He peeled it off, followed by his trousers and picked everything up before placing it in the washing basket.

"Come to Daddy little miss, let's get you all

cleaned up," Harvey said, picking up Millie, realizing that she had fallen asleep.

"Huh?" Millie said, opening her eyes and looking around, turning her body slightly in Harvey's arms as he held her while the bath water ran. He lit scented candles and added bath salts to the warm water of the spa bath before carefully stepping in with Millie still in his arms. Sitting down in the water, Millie snuggled into his chest, and he poured coconut and shea butter body lotion over Millie's tits, soaping her up in a thick lather, letting her tits bounce out of his hands, pulling them back up by her nipples as she sleepily rested in his arms. Taking his time to rub her cunt, not wanting to hurt her and understanding how sensitive she still was by how swollen she still was.

"Daddy, can I please stay the night?" Millie suddenly asked, turning to look up at him, her wide eyes looking at him innocently causing his heart to flutter.

"Yes, baby girl. Daddy wasn't going to let you go tonight, don't worry," Harvey said, pouring warm water over her body, rinsing her off.

"But are you going to be a good girl and let Daddy dress you?" Harvey asked, wondering how far she would let him go. Millie just nodded her head, deep in the little space she hadn't realized was too close to the surface.

"Come on then, the water is starting to get a cold little one," Harvey said, taking Millie by the hand and leading her out of the bath. He took down a fluffy black towel and dried her off, kissing her softly as he patted the water droplets off her body.

"Take Daddy's hand," Harvey said and waited for Millie to obey before walking her back to his bed.

"Lay down little one," he instructed, watching as Millie lowered herself on top of his sheets, her body being swallowed up by the marshmallow-like quilt and pillows. Harvey took out baby powder, a bunny print diaper and doubled the lining he usually would have used. He placed them down on the bed before going back to the cupboard and opening up a draw of onesies. He chose a baby pink long sleeved onesies that had a bunny print on the front to match the diaper he was going to put Millie in and a black pacifier. He took out black thigh high socks and walked back to the bed.

"Alright little girl, let's get you ready for bed," Harvey said grabbing Millie by her hips and pulling her body down to the edge of the bed and towards his cock which to Millie's surprise was hard again.

"Daddy I don't think I can," Millie said, bringing her hands to cover her pussy, thinking that Harvey was going to fuck her again. He laughed and leaned over her, his cock pressing into her hands as he kissed her face all over.

"Teddy isn't going to play with you again little one, don't worry, he knows when you can't play anymore," Harvey said taking her hands away and placing them above her head. He took the diaper and gently slapped Millie's thighs.

"Lift your bottom, baby," he instructed and

waited for Millie to follow his direction. He placed the diaper under her bottom, enjoying her surprised face at how it felt. He placed a hand on her chest as she tried to rest on her elbows, pushing her back down.

"Stay still for Daddy," he said, moving his hands, making her tits to jiggle as she felt the powered sprinkle over her pussy for the first time. He pulled the diaper tight, the thickness of the padding soft against her sensitive pussy.

"Such a pretty girl," Harvey said, taking the onesie and pulling it over Millie's head and wriggling it down her body, enjoying how she looked rolling around the bed in her diaper. Millie giggled as Harvey took her wrists in his hands and pulled her arms into the sleeves of the soft outfit.

"One last thing," Harvey said, pushing the pacifier into Millie's mouth, slapping her cheek gently when she tried to refuse him.

"Don't be bad for Daddy little girl," Harvey said, running his hands over Millie's thickly diapered pussy. Millie moaned behind her paci and wriggled against Harvey's touch as he tickled her all over.

"Daddy stop it," Millie giggled, her little voice making Harvey lick his lips. He got up and pulled on his long pajama sweats before climbing in bed with Millie.

"Come and cuddle Daddy," he said, pulling her to him, patting her between her splayed thighs as she began to fall asleep.

Chapter 5

"Who is a pretty baby?" Willow said brushing Millie's hair back, stroking her forehead. Millie opened her sleepy eyes and was startled by the black haired woman lying next to her.

"Shh little girl, it is ok," Willow said, pulling Millie into her arms, easily overpowering a resisting Millie. Forgetting she had a paci in her mouth, Millie tried to speak but as her words came out as incoherent mumble, making Willow laughed cruelly.

"Oh sweetie, I don't understand your baby talk," Willow said, placing her hand over the top of Millie's mouth making holding her head in place.

"What? Don't you want a Mama as well as a Daddy little girl?" Willow teased, wrapping her legs around Millie's and forcing them open as she rubbed Millie's diaper covered pussy. Millie tried to look for Harvey but couldn't see him.

"Daddy has gone out little girl; he won't be back for a while. Guess you will have to stay with Mama until he gets back," Willow said cruelly as she stroked Millie.

"Didn't he tell you about me little one?" Willow said, looking down to see Millie's tear-filled eyes. Millie shook her head but settled into Willow's arms. Feeling another woman's breasts for the first time, as Willow pressed herself against Millie's face.

"Well that was rude of him," Willow said annoyed that she hadn't been given a mention.

"Regardless, if I let you go, will you be a good girl for Mama?" Willow said. Millie took in the dark beauty of the woman who had so boldly forced herself on her and felt silly for being so naïve. *Of course, he already has a girlfriend*, Millie thought sadly, but she just nodded her head and looked down, embarrassed to be dressed like this in front of the stunningly attractive and powerful woman. Willow placed both her hands on the side of Millie's cheeks and softened more than she realized she could as she thumbed away the tears that fell from Millie's eyes.

"Shh baby, it's ok, Mama is going to take care of you," Willow said, kissing Millie's cheeks before taking the paci from Millie's mouth.

"There, little Millie, what a sweet girl you are," Willow said, smiling kindly at Millie.

"Um, I think I should go," Millie softly said, trying to get up. Willow sat back and watched as Millie began to take her onesie off, pulling at the clips between her legs, her fingers fumbling to get them open. Willow rolled her eyes and placed her hands over the top of Millie's.

"Let Mama," Willow said, pushing Millie onto her back. Millie breathed deeply as Willow ripped the clips open in one quick motion and began running her hands up Millie's body, pulling the onesie off as she went. Stopping just under Millie's big tits, Willow bent down and kissed Millie's soft tummy making Millie tighten her abs and try to pull away from Willow.

"You'll have to get used to Mama touching you little one. Have you ever been touch by a woman before?" Willow asked, the answer already evident by the reluctant consent Millie was giving her. Millie shook her head no, unable to speak as Willow decided to keep Millie's tits covered. She came to lay next to Millie once again, this time making Millie's eyes go wide as she was frozen by what she saw. Willow unzipped her black bomber jacket exposing her E-cup natural looking but fake tits nestled in a dark red lace bra. Millie watched, almost captivated as Willow let her coat fall to the side, never breaking eye contact with Millie as she reached around and unhooked her bra.

"Do you like what you see little girl, are you hungry for Mama?" Willow asked, pulling the bottom of Millie's onesie back down and doing the clips up again.

"Uh uh little girl, don't get fussy for Mama," Willow said as Millie reached down and tried to push her hands away. Willow stared Millie down with her piercing green eyes until Millie took her hands away, her head spinning by having another woman treat her like this. Willow moved up to the head of the bed and sat against it, patting her lap seductively.

"Come here, princess," she cooed, excited to have Millie obey her so willingly. Millie lay down on Willow's lap, facing up and looking into Willow's captivating eyes, opening her mouth involuntarily as Willow bent forward and rubbed her nipple across Millie's lips.

"What did Daddy teach you little one?" Willow said, stroking Millie's tummy before patting her diapered pussy.

"To suck whatever he put in my mouth," Millie said quietly making Willow smile.

"Then open wide bubba," Willow said. Millie parted her lips just as she felt Willow's nipple pressing into her mouth and began sucking the older woman's nipple. Willow moaned at how soft Millie's tongue was and bent her knees up to roll Millie into her, patting her ass and uncovered thighs.

"Such a good girl," Willow said, surprised at how loving she felt towards Millie. *This was not the fucking plan*; she thought to herself as she moved her arm to cradle Millie who continued to suckle from her. Enjoying a tender moment with Millie, Willow stroked her cheek as she sucked, smiling lovingly at Millie when she made little noises. Millie was surprised she liked what was happening to her, and she brought her hands up to hold Willow's heavy breast in her hands. Willow bent down to kiss Millie's forehead in delighted bliss as she saw how Millie's hands looked small on her tit and repositioned herself, so Millie didn't have to hold the weight of it all herself.

"We have such sweet girl," Willow said victoriously as she looked up and saw Harvey walking towards the open bedroom door. He was carrying a shopping bag and placed it at the entrance of the room as he looked in. Rage was the first emotion he felt. Anger that Willow was holding his baby girl, rage at whatever she had done to convince Millie to be in that position. He knew it couldn't have been Millie's fault; she was sweet and new and innocent. Willow, on the other hand, he knew to be wicked. Harvey came and sat next to Willow and looked down into Millie's eyes. He smiled at her before kissing her on her nose, deciding that it was better to punish Willow in private, he didn't want to scare Millie off by what he was already planning to do to Willow.

"She is a good girl, aren't you, baby?" Harvey said taking Millie in his arms and off Willow's breast. He held her close, taking her paci and placing it back in her mouth before walking her out to the living room.

"Just wait here little one, Daddy just needs a minute," he said, turning on some cartoons for Millie and stroking her hair before going back into the bedroom. When he entered, Willow was redressing herself, slowly zipping up her jacket.

"Cute baby we have, Daddy," Willow said her voice full of challenge. Harvey just closed the door quietly behind him, locking it before turning around and backhanding Willow cross the face, causing her to fall to the floor.

"What the fuck are you playing at bitch?" He hissed in a low tone, burning with rage. Willow opened her mouth to speak, but Harvey slapped her again, grabbing her hair and lifting her to her feet before throwing her back onto the bed. He jumped on top of her and pinned her down, sitting on top of her with his thighs on either side of her waist.

"She wasn't complaining; I guess she's not your perfect baby after all," Willow hissed back copping another slap this time on the other side of her face.

"Is this what you wanted? Did you want to be punished? You didn't want me to let you go, so you try and compromise her?" Harvey said, placing his hand on Willow's throat.

"I just thought maybe you'd want both of us," Willow said as Harvey tightened his grip on her neck. He loosened it in disgust, angry at her and angry at himself for thinking that she could have accepted a clean break. Harvey got off her and walked into the bathroom, looking at himself in the mirror.

"It felt nice, you know, to care for someone. To hold her," Willow said, coming in behind him and placing a hand on his back. He flinched, not wanting to feel what he was feeling. If he had been honest with himself, he would have told Willow he never wanted to lose her. That he had loved fucking her ragged, but that he needed a softer woman as his baby girl. She was the temptress men dream about. The slut that never said no, that was always willing and ready that can seduce even the most loyal man until he is balls deep in her cunt. The power-hungry executive with the heels that conditioned everyone to fear her presence. And Harvey knew it, he knew he loved her for her power and dominance, but he also knew that she was never going to the baby he wanted and he was angry at himself for not having realized this sooner.

"I must admit, I was shocked at how motherly you looked," he said, looking in the mirror at Willow's reflection. She smirked.

"I wasn't prepared for that either," she said, showing him a softer side.

"She's straight, how did you get her to be so relaxed with you?" Harvey said, turning around, for the first time looking at the damage he had done to her face. Frowning, he wet the corner of a washcloth and pressed it to her cheek. Willow just narrowed her eyes and took the cloth from him, holding it to her face.

"I would have done the same, don't worry," she said. Harvey watched as she moved to sit down on the edge of the bath.

"I told her that Daddy had gone out and that Mama was going to look after her. She was very confused," Willow said, clearly impressed with herself. Harvey laughed and came to sit next to her.

"And?" He prompted knowing that there was more to the story.

"I said Daddy was silly for not telling her about me and that she should get used to Mama touching her," Willow said, shrugging her shoulders.

"I'm just sexy, what can I say, baby girl loved Mama's big titties," Willow joked rubbing her hands over her breasts and bouncing them in her hands.

"So, you want to play happy families?" He said, passing her the soothing balm for her red face and neck. Willow sat and thought before standing up and walking towards the bedroom door.

"Yeah," she said winking as she unlocked the door and walked down the hallway.

"Where's Mama's good girl?" Willow called out making Harvey jump to his feet and follow her out into the living room. Millie had been watching the cartoons Harvey had left on for her as Willow sat down next to her and wrapped her arm and Millie.

"Such a sweetheart," Willow said as Harvey came to sit on Millie's other side.

"Daddy," Millie said, snuggling into him.

Millie wrapped her arms around Harvey's waist, and he felt his heart soften instantly.

"Oh baby girl," he said, picking her up and placing her on his lap. Millie rested her head on his shoulder as he rocked her gently, Willow moving closer to sit next to him. Placing her hand on his crotch, Harvey put Millie to one side and away from Willow's hands.

"Mama, what are you doing?" Millie suddenly said making Willow smirk and look up.

"I'm going to make Daddy happy, baby girl, do you want to watch or not?" Willow said more gently than Harvey had ever heard her speak before. He frowned as he thought about all the times he had tried to get Willow to show a softer side, surprised that it had been his baby girl who had made it happen. Willow suddenly pulled his cock from his pants and began sucking, ripping him out of his daydream and causing him to gasp.

"I guess you're going to watch little one," Willow said, stopping briefly to smile wickedly at Millie. Millie, feeling uncomfortable with the situation, took out her paci suddenly and stood up, as though snapping out of the daze she had been in since arriving at Harvey's house the day before.

"I've got to go," she said, running into his bedroom and locking the door behind her before he had the chance to stop her.

"Millie, open up baby," Harvey said banging on the door. There was desperation in his voice, not wanting to lose her. Millie took off her onesie, diaper, and socks before going to the bathroom and showering. She hadn't heard Harvey take an axe and break through his bedroom door, but as she left the bathroom with just her towel, she saw him standing in the room holding the axe.

"Harvey, please don't," Millie said, instantly scared that he would hurt her. Frowning in confusion before realizing what she was afraid of, Harvey dropped the axe.

"Oh no no Millie, I just used it to break the door down. You're ok; you're safe, Millie. I'm not going to hurt you," he said to Millie who had begun to cry.

"It's just all too much; I can't. Please let me go home," Millie said softly and looking into her towel. Harvey sat on the edge of his bed and looked down to the floor.

"Yeah I'm sorry, I shouldn't have left this morning, this isn't the way I wanted it to go down," he said, shaking his head.

"You should have just told me about her, I've never been with a woman, but like, I've never called someone Daddy or wore a diaper either, I would have been cool with it if you have just told me," Millie said looking around for her clothes. Harvey had washed and ironed them before he had gone to buy breakfast and got up, remembering where he had got them from.

"Millie, she shouldn't have even been here. We aren't together. I let her stay here when her ex kicked her out, and we had just been fucking for a while. I'm not with her, and in fact, she had been looking for a new place to move into," Harvey said, passing Millie her clothes. Millie just shook her head as she got dressed, trying to process what he was telling her.

"She was just trying to get back at me for telling her that she had to move out, I'm so sorry she has done this to you," Harvey said taking the towel from Millie and placing it in the bathroom.

"Harvey, I just can't," Millie said, placing her hand on his chest before leaving the room. Harvey nodded, understanding that things had gone way too far and stayed in the room, not wanting to make it any harder for Millie to leave.

"Going so soon, baby girl?" Willow said seeing Millie walk towards the door. Millie just looked at her, her broken-heart eyes catching Willow off guard who softened immediately.

"Hey look, I'm sorry," Willow said, standing up and hurrying over to where Millie stood.

"Don't," Millie said as Willow placed both her hands on Millie's shoulders forcing her to face her.

"Millie, Harvey is a great guy, I shouldn't have done that, I'm sorry," Willow said catching the tear that escaped Millie's eyes and pulling her to her chest, embracing her, surprised that the younger woman could make her feel so moved.

"Please, just let me go," Millie said, pushing Willow away gently, breaking the embrace and turning to walk out the front door.

Chapter 6

"Are you going to get out of bed?" Willow asked Harvey who had stayed in bed for the last two days. He thought back to how he had tried to introduce Millie to his world, how hot Willow and her had looked, how he wished he hadn't gone so far with her so quickly. He had sent her nine messages and hadn't got a reply from one of them. He had even gone to the bar that they had met last week. *That's it, it hasn't even been longer than seven days, and I'm already ruined by her, fuck*, he thought throwing a pillow at Willow who was standing in his doorway. He hadn't bothered to fix the hack job he did on the door.

"No," was all he bothered to say. Willow looked at him with pity in her eyes.

"This is pathetic; you do know that, right?" She said viciously. He didn't want to hear it, throwing another pillow in her direction.

"Fuck off," he said, wondering how she had become the one with reason and logic. He knew she was right, which irritated him.

"Why are you still in my house?" He suddenly asked, wondering what it would take for her to leave.

"Oh, you love me being here, who else is going to train all your pretty clients and keep your business alive while you have your tantrum?" Willow smirked, remembering how a blonde with a thick booty licked her pussy when she sat on her face.

"What?" Harvey asked, confused. Willow just rolled her eyes and came to sit next to him on his bed.

"Well, while you have been in here, I've been out there, training and fucking your pretty little clients. Don't worry; they've loved it. I told them I'm your new assistant," Willow said, clearly impressed with herself. Harvey just pulled the blankets over his head and groaned.

"Do you know how long I have worked to get that all up and running and you are just coming in and fucking with it?" He said, hiding under the blankets. Willow smirked to herself before getting up and walking out of the room.

"Hey, I wasn't finished feeling sorry for myself," Harvey called out to her, deciding that he needed to get up and get to work before she fucked his business into the ground.

Millie had been numb since she left Harvey's home. She had done the usual things, gone to work, exercised at the gym and tried to bring herself down from the whirlwind weekend she had experienced at Harvey's. Everything about her time with him made her head spin. The care that he had taken with her, seeming to know just how far to push and pull her, the way that he was fully present when she was talking to him, and then there was Willow. *She is just a whole other level I'm not even getting into right now*, Millie thought, dismissing the memory of Willow's overwhelmingly seductive presence.

Looking out the window, Millie saw her reflection as the bus drove through a tunnel. Her sad eyes made her own heart, ache at the image of a woman she hardly recognized. Looking away and out into the mass of people all blankly staring back at her. *I wonder if they can see it, see what I've done, see what he did, and see what I let him do. See what she did*, Millie thought blushing as she remembered how it felt to be diapered and given a paci to suck. Quickly turning back to stare out the window, she squeezed her eyes shut as to try and push the memory from her mind and out of her heart. Failing, she dipped her head and let the images of Willow's huge breast and Harvey's kind eyes as he pushed his cock deep inside of her relentlessly, using her until he was satisfied but making her feel safer than she ever had flood her mind.

"Hey, you need to speak with Harvey," Millie heard a voice say behind her. She was buying groceries and had reached up to take a packet of cake mix down from the top shelf, having to stand on her tippy toes to reach. Turning around, Willow was standing behind her, her hands on her hips of her skinny black jeans, her cream heels tapping a toe impatiently. Millie just looked at her. With her beige trench coat and V-neck black sweater, her eyes were more piercing than Millie remembered, seeing Willow's sensual smoky eye and perfect highlight rendering her speechless.

"I don't know what to say to him," Millie softly finally said to which Willow just laughed.

"How about, hey Daddy I miss you come back to me?" Willow said causing Millie to try and hush her as she looked around the store frantically, hoping that no-one had heard Willow who just smirked in amusement.

"Do you miss him?" Willow suddenly asked, wondering if she had missed something.

"Yes, of course," Millie said defensively before realizing what she had said and reflected on her words.

"Well then little girl," Willow teased holding out her hand to Millie.

"What?" Millie said, wondering what Willow wanted. Willow just rolled her eyes and reached down taking Millie's hand in hers.

"That's no way to speak to Mama," Willow said, enjoying Millie's discomfort.

"You're not my Mama," Millie muttered stubbornly making Willow laugh.

"True, however," Willow said, turning Millie around to look at her, suddenly becoming very serious.

"Harvey does miss you, and if it hadn't been for my, games shall we say, you two would be happily playing house instead of feeling miserable. Millie, he cares about you. I've never seen him so destroyed by a woman before, and I kinda think you haven't had a guy like him before and maybe that's exactly what you need," Willow said speaking candidly, making Millie feel the truth of her words in the pit of her being.

"He's over there sweetie, go and talk to

him," Willow almost pleaded. She watched Millie as she slowly turned to see Harvey trying to decide which pasta to buy, reading both labels at the same time. Millie turned back to Willow, who placed her two fingers to Millie's lips when she began to speak.

"Go!" Willow said, practicing her Mama voice on Millie who was taken aback by how commanding Willow sounded.

"Yes Ma'ma," Millie muttered gaining a slap on her ass as she passed Willow who stood by Millie's shopping trolley feeling very impressed with her matchmaking abilities.

"It doesn't matter which one you buy; they are both shit. Get this one instead," Millie said as confidently as she could fake, holding up the most expensive packet of pasta she had quickly found. Harvey looked up, surprised to be seeing Millie standing in front of him.

"Hi," she said softly, tucking her hair behind her ear. Harvey just looked at her like she had answered his most troubling question, shaking his head to try and keep the conversation alive.

"Um, hi," was all that he could manage before he started smiling like a schoolboy.

"You're speaking with me," he gushed, blushing slightly. Millie smiled at her feet, her feelings for Harvey flooding her veins in the strongest pull she had ever felt.

"Yeah well, I couldn't let you buy that rubbish. And also, I was afraid of what Willow would do to me if I didn't talk to you," Millie said, laughing looking up to see Willow walking over to the pair.

"You're welcome. Now off you go, go do some Daddy baby girl activities together and live happily ever after," she said, laughing to herself and placing all Millie's groceries into Harvey's shopping trolley.

"What? Are you going to let her starve?" Willow asked Harvey who was looking at her in a panic.

"Millie, it's ok I don't expect you to," Harvey said, being surprised he was cut off by Millie who just placed her fingers to his lips.

"Shh, Daddy," Millie softly said, taking the pasta from his hands and dropping it into the trolley as well, beaming cheekily up at him.

"I'm glad that worked. My next thought was to hold the photos of you to ransom," Willow said, making both Harvey and Millie spin around and look at her.

"What photos?!" They both asked, Harvey, shaking his head wondering what damage Willow was trying to do next.

"These," Willow said showing Millie a photo of herself, the morning she had woken up with Willow sitting next to her.

"You have to delete them, please Willow," Millie begged in a hushed voice as someone passed them. Willow stared her down, pleasantly surprised when Millie refused to back down.

"Oh baby girl, you've got some steel under that soft shell. Here, look it's gone. Which is a real shame because you looked adorable!" Willow said teasingly.

"Is she out of the house?" Millie asked Harvey, who laughed at her direct tone.

"Yes, Millie, she is. She left two days after, you know, everything turned to shit," Harvey said, regret in his voice. Millie took his hand and snuggled into his chest, feeling his arms close around her, and she melted into him, feeling at home again.

Chapter 7

Millie met Harvey in a café close to her apartment by the park a week later. She had read up on the frenzied headspace that many new people in the kink community experience and related more to the articles than she wished she had. She had joined forums and groups online that addressed differing elements of the DDlg dynamic and enjoyed learning more about the fluidity of sexuality. She also learned about how some people had MDlg dynamics that were completely no sexual, and she wondered if that was what she wanted to experience with Willow. Quickly deciding that Willow would have fucked her if time had been on her side, Millie laughed to herself and shook her head.

"Hey there sweetie," Harvey said, rushing in. It was raining, and Millie had arrived early, worried that the buses would run late due to the weather. She watched as Harvey took his coat off and ran his fingers through his semi-dry hair, making sure that the style was still maintained.

"You look good, Daddy," Millie said reassuringly in his ear as she passed him and went to get the order she had placed earlier.

"Clever girl," Harvey said when Millie came back and placed his coffee in front of him. Millie smiled and looked into his eyes.

"What are you having?" Harvey asked curiously, peering into her glass. Millie had started drinking green juices for breakfast, and Harvey noticed that she had lost some of her softness. Today though, she was not holding back and had ordered a caramel fudge latte with extra cream and sprinkles.

"It's called the Rocket, I guess because it sends your sugar levels over the moon," Millie said making Harvey laugh.

"This is nice. Thank you for being so open to this and us. I'm truly sorry about how it all started," Harvey said, shaking his head before sipping his black coffee. He took the biscuit that had come with his coffee and scooped up some cream from Millie's drink on the edge.

"Tasty," he said before going back for more. Millie sat back in her chair and looked at Harvey. He met her eyes and kept her gaze, staying in that moment in time with her, letting the rest of the world fade away. Millie couldn't remember a time when everything had fallen so utterly into place. The sun broke through the clouds, beaming into the café and onto their faces, making both of them squint but continue to look at each other.

"Let's do this," Millie said, standing up and holding out her hand to Harvey.

"Where are we going?" Harvey asked, enjoying following Millie out of the café, flicking up his coat with one hand.

"I've seen your place, but you haven't seen mine," Millie said hailing a taxi impressing Harvey with her wolf whistle.

"Yeah, I've got some tricks, Daddy," Millie

said cheekily winking at him. Harvey grinned back at her but didn't respond; he was just enjoying falling into her world.

The taxi took them 15 blocks away from the city and to the edge of a nature reserve and into the driveway of a small white apartment building with a white picket fence, and red rose bushes in full bloom out the front.

"Wow, this is lovely baby," Harvey said, paying the taxi driver catching Millie off guard.

"Oh, I hope that was ok, I just," Harvey said, not wanting to push Millie too far again.

"No it's nice, I just wasn't expecting it. I like that you take care of things like that, Daddy," Millie said, opening her gate and being greeted by a large black cat.

"I hope you're not allergic, Daddy," Millie said, scratching the cat behind the ears before walking up to the door.

"She's not mine, she's sort of like the neighborhoods, that's why she's so fat," Millie laughed as the cat walked into her apartment as though she owned it.

"That's funny. No, I'm not allergic to anything," Harvey said, looking around Millie's homely country style home.

"You have exquisite taste," Harvey said, sitting down on her Chesterfield couch and spreading his arms out along the back of the leather.

"I'm glad you like it," Millie said, turning the heating on.

"Do you want a drink or anything?" Millie asked as Harvey jumped up and walked into her kitchen behind her. He placed his hands on her hips and pressed play on the playlist he had made for her, swaying her hips in time with his, pressing into her.

"Daddy," Millie said, feeling her body grow warm in anticipation. Harvey twirled her before bringing her close to him again.

"Yes?" He playfully asked, cupping her breasts in his hands over her soft, fluffy light yellow sweater.

"These look so good. Let Daddy have a little look," Harvey said, lifting the sweater slightly and seeing that Millie's bra matched. He reached roughly into her bra and pulled her tits out, making them rest over her bra, flicking her nipples until he had made them so sensitive that Millie pulled away from him. Laughing he reached around and unhooked her bra and pulled the straps down, throwing her bra on the floor and rubbing her tits over her sweater he had pulled back down.

"Daddy doesn't want you wearing a bra when it's just you and I in either of our houses. Is that ok princess?" Harvey asked Millie.

"Yes, Daddy," Millie replied as Harvey sat down at her kitchen table and pulled her onto his lap. He took his time groping her, having missed playing with her. Millie just rested her head back on his shoulder and stuck out her chest, giving him full access to what he desired. It didn't surprise her that she felt him growing under her skirt sooner rather than later, feeling him shift her on his lap, taking his predatory hands away only to reach under her skirt and spread her ass cheeks either side of his cock.

"You'll feel it sticking into your pussy soon little girl, will you let Daddy fuck today?" Harvey whispered in Millie's ear as he went back to using his hands on her tits, enjoying his intentional degrading. He liked that he felt like a dirty older man preying on his young victim, Millie's ever eager submission to him driving him wild.

"Yes, Daddy," Millie gasped as she did feel Harvey's huge cock tilt up and press into her slit. He grunted as he lifted her off his lap enough to force her to take his cock sliding back and forth along her already wet slit.

"I'm happy you didn't wear any panties like Daddy told you. You're a good girl, aren't you Millie?" Harvey said, pulling at her skirt.

"Take it off," he instructed. Millie stood up and began swinging her hips in time with the music, twirling on the spot and slowly unzipping the back of her skirt in front of Harvey. She spread her thighs and straddled his leg as she undid the skirt entirely and let it drop on the floor, her naked pussy beginning to grind on his thigh in time to the music. Harvey leaned back and watched as her ass bounced and jiggled on him, slapping her thighs and taking the small butt plug from his pocket.

"Bend forward," he commanded, slapping her ass one final time. He spat on the plug and began pushing it into Millie's ass, making her gasp and moan.

"Keep it in," Harvey said as Millie reached back around her ass and spread her cheeks to adjust the plug inside her comfortably.

"Daddy's, precious little princess," Harvey said, standing up, making Millie do the same.

"Show Daddy where we are playing, baby girl," he said, gripping Millie on the back of her neck and picking up his bag as she led him to her bedroom.

He threw her onto her bed and took in the room. It had soft furnishings, a fireplace, and thick pink fur rug on the floor. Harvey took out three black satin ties and draped them over Millie's tummy.

"Take your sweater off, little one," he instructed, lighting a fire before turning around to see that Millie had followed his instruction.

"Good," he said, looking at her unmarked skin. Harvey took one of the ties and began tying up Millie's tits, starting on the left side, he grabbed at her and pulled her tit out towards him.

"Ripe and ready to be taken aren't you," he said enjoying how Millie's breast became hard, her nipple poking out as he tied one and then the other.

"Look at you," he said, standing back and looking at his handy work. He had tied Millie so that her wrists were bound behind her back and her tits were forced out from her chest, on display for his enjoyment. Touching her, he smirked as she shuddered when he ran his fingernails over the tops of her tits, the skin being pulled tight.

"I'm going to enjoy those," Harvey said as he brought both his hands down to slap them, making Millie scream.

"Hmm, you might be a bit too loud, let Daddy fix that," Harvey said looking into his bag and pulling out a dildo gag like the one Millie had shown him a photo of.

"Does this look familiar? Daddy knows how you like to suck cock; now you can while I play with you," he said, pushing the soft object into her mouth and down her throat.

"Now, where was I, oh yes," Harvey said, picking Millie up and placing her on her knees on her pink rug. He sat on the edge of the bed and slowly took off his shoes, followed by his belt, jeans, and briefs.

"Have you missed Teddy, baby girl? He has missed you," Harvey said, reaching forward and pulling Millie close to him as he began to rub his cock over her big tits in their firm restraints. Millie felt his touch more intensely and moaned as she closed her eyes and sucked on the dildo strapped to her mouth.

"Yeah, Daddy's dirty girl," Harvey said as he flicked her nipples with his pre-cumming cock, making her nipples wet and sticky. He grabbed two handfuls of Millie's bound breasts and pulled her closer again as he slid his cock between her helpless tits.

"Daddy is going to cover you in cum," Harvey said as he began fucking Millie's tits roughly, reaching under the tie and holding it firmly in one hand as he slid up and down her deep crease, her nipples shaking as he thrust hard and came over the tops of her tits.

"Oh yeah, Daddy gave you those porn star titties. You gonna be my little porn star tonight, baby girl," Harvey said as he pushed her onto her back and kneed over her, fucking her tits again. This time he knew where he wanted to cum and took the gag from Millie's mouth, covering her mouth with his hand, not interested in hearing her moans. He felt his balls get full and his cock surge as he groped one of Millie's tits as he fucked her helpless body before taking his hand away and pushing his cock down her throat, cumming in her as she gagged and choked on his monster.

"Yeah, that's what I expect from my baby girl, that you take what Daddy gives you without complaining," Harvey said picking her up and placing her on his lap and down on his cock. Millie gasped as she was unexpectedly filled, Harvey cumming again inside her. He bounced her on his lap, watching as her bound tits bounced and jiggled, his cum dripping from her nipples. Millie felt him more intensely with the plug in her ass and knew that she was close to her limit. Harvey could feel it too as she became quiet.

"Daddy's good girl," he said cumming one last time before quickly untying her, her tits feeling blood flow back into them and her wrists getting pins and needles as he rubbed them lovingly.

"I loved that, Daddy," Millie said, surprised that she had been the one to suggest most of the scene, the previous week.

Chapter 8

Harvey knew what he wanted as he watched Millie sleep in her bed. This time after their night together, he hadn't left. Instead, he had made a coffee, gone back to bed and watched Millie as she curled up in the blankets. She had rolled into his lap and he re-positioned his legs so that she was laying between them, her mouth close to his cock. Drinking his coffee as he stroked Millie's hair, he pressed his cock covered sweat pants to her lips, smirking as she pouted her lips in a kiss. Feeling it wiggle with excitement, he reached into his pants and took it out, jerking his balls in one hand and holding Millie's head down on his lap as he rubbed his hardening cock against her soft cheek. Pressing the tip down as it formed its hard shaft, Harvey rubbed the tip over her lips, groaning in anticipation as her lips were forced open around the top.

"Suck," Harvey whispered lovingly, pulling on his sack as Millie opened her mouth and he pushed into her, past her teeth to the soft stop he wanted and slowly pulled back out.

"Good girl," he said, taking her face in both his hands as he face fucked her awake. He knew he'd have to hold her down as her eyes opened and she startled, trying to pull away from him, he just pushed into her further, forcing her throat open.

"Take it," Harvey roughly growled, holding her face to his balls, his cock throbbing down her neck as he squirted into her. Millie's eyes watered with the sensation and he held the back of her head to him as his other hand reached under the blankets to toy with her cunt.

"Don't you dare try and take it out, you'll take Daddy when and how I want, remember, princess?" Harvey warned, reminding Millie of the commitment she had made to him. She just nodded as the dick she had in her mouth prevented her from being able to speak.

"Yeah, I bet you do," Harvey said as he went back to thrusting his rod down her throat. Taking his cock out suddenly, Millie gasped for air as he turned her over and ripped the bed sheets back. He took her by her hips, picked her up, and pushed her against a wall, fucking her in the air.

"I'm going to carry you around the house all day with Teddy buried deep inside of you. You're going to be locked into Daddy, unable to escape every pump of my cock I want to fill you with," Harvey whispered as Millie wrapped her arms around his head and tried to lift off him as her orgasm ravaged her. Harvey just laughed as he stuck his thumb in her ass suddenly, making her gasp and try to wiggle away from him.

"What did Daddy just say?" He said, holding Millie slightly away from him and humping her roughly, wanting to empty his load in her as he anchored her to him with his thumb starting to wiggle inside her making her moaning as she was taken with primal force.

"Yeah, that's it, cum for Daddy, little girl," Harvey said, as Millie panted. He had taken her around to the kitchen as he placed her on her back on the counter and watched as his cock filled her, pushing her tummy out with each pump, cream dripping down her thighs.

"Daddy's not finished yet," Harvey said, picking her back up and keeping his cock pounding her as he walked to the living room and roughly threw her down on the couch. Grabbing her ankles, he held her legs open as he pulled her cunt to him, sliding his cock in balls deep, again before leaning over her and driving his massive shaft into her, drilling her hard.

"Turn around," he said, pulling out of her and turning her around. He slapped her bubble butt, taking two hand-fills and shaking it.

"Shake your ass for Daddy," Harvey instructed as Millie got to her knees and twerked for him as he placed the tip of his wet cock into her ass, making her groan.

"I didn't say stop," he said, grabbing her

ponytail and roughly pulling her head back to look at him. He slapped her ass repeatedly; he stuffed her ass with his cock as she twerked for him. Making her scream as she was stretched, Harvey continued to spank her ass red, enjoying the whimpers she began to gasp.

"You like this don't you, this is what you need," Harvey said, putting two fingers in Millie's mouth, fish hooking her as he slowly fucked her ass.

"Yes, Daddy," Millie said around the big fingers filling her mouth.

"Oh I just want to stuff all your holes," Harvey said, pumping her ass harder while his free hand stopped spanking her and reached under her and into her used cunt.

"I wonder if Daddy can fist you, little girl," Harvey said quickly slipping three fingers inside Millie. He knew he didn't have long to play when she began to resist him, her pussy clenching and her head trying to shake his fingers from her mouth. Forcefully, he stuffed another finger inside of her as she came hard, falling limp on the couch as he finished his onslaught, fucking her long enough to remind her that he was in charge, but softly enough for her to know that he cared for her. Pulling out of her ass, cunt, and mouth all at once, Millie felt empty as Harvey dumped his load onto her tits, fucking them as he held them together in his big hands. He was sliding his still throbbing cock up and down the soft tunnel he had made.

"Yeah, you're just for Daddy aren't you," Harvey said as he came again, cum squirting up and around her neck, dribbling back down onto the tops of her tits. Standing up and looking down on his baby girl, Harvey smiled at how she had taken him. Her holes are dripping cum onto herself, her hair a mess, her ass red, her tits covered in his cream.

"Pretty girl," Harvey said, picking her up gently, holding her tenderly in his arms.

"Have I fucked you good, little girl," Harvey said, walking her to the bath.

"But now I want more," he added, making Millie's eyes go wide.

"I don't think I can take anymore, Daddy," Millie said, worried at what Harvey wanted with her body now. Harvey just laughed as he ran the bath water for Millie.

"No, little one, Daddy wants his baby girl back. Not the little slut I just used like I'd paid for her," Harvey said, lowering Millie into the warm water. He left the bathroom, returning with bubble bath and bath ducks.

"Do you like duckies little one?" He asked, watching as Millie entered her little space.

"Yeah, Daddy," she excitedly said, clapping her hands. Harvey washed her body clean as Millie played with the toys before taking her out and drying her off.

"Daddy, I hurt here," Millie said, referring to her ass. Harvey just nodded and took her hand as he led her to the bedroom. He picked the blankets he had thrown on the floor and lay Millie down on top as he took out a puffy white diaper.

"I bet it does, you were such a good girl for Daddy, let me have a look," Harvey said opening a tub of thick, soothing balm and gently rubbing it over Millie's ass-hole.

"It might hurt for a little while, but Daddy will keep looking after it, ok?" Harvey asked Millie who could only nod. He had given her a pink paci, happy that Millie was such an obedient girl. He sprinkled the powder over her pussy, rubbing it in so she wouldn't chaff and tighten the tabs around her waist.

"Daddy wants to go out for brunch today, so, you'll have to wear some big girl clothes, but you'll keep your diapy on," Harvey said, slapping Millie's thighs as she tried to speak.

"I didn't ask what you wanted, it doesn't matter, you are Daddy's little girl, and you'll do as you're told," Harvey said firmly. He went to Millie's cupboard and looked through her clothes. Selecting a pair of black stockings, a black pinafore dress and a white T-shirt he walked back over to were Millie was rolling around on the bed, enjoying the feeling of the thick padding pushing her thighs open, exposing her to Harvey who rubbed her lustfully.

"Such a pretty girl," He said, and she knew that he wanted to fuck her again. He carefully rolled the stockings over her toes and up her calves, stopping and standing back, enjoying how she looked, her thighs being forced to close around the thick padding he knew would be rubbing on her clit and pussy.

"Do you like your diapy, baby girl?" Harvey asked, going back to her cupboard and taking out a light pink bra.

"It'll match your paci, everyone will think you are so cute," Harvey said stroking her face with his index finger before sitting her up, holding her as her abs ached and she winced in pain.

"Shh, Daddy's got you," Harvey said filling the cups of her bra with her juicy tits, making them bounce as he pulled on the straps, delighting his cock which moved in desire. Going back, Harvey continued to roll the stockings up Millie's thighs and over her thick diaper, making it squish into her as he secured the stockings over it. He took her T-shirt and carefully pulled it over her head and ran his hands over her tits as he covered them with the tight shirt.

"Crawl to Daddy," he instructed, sitting back and watching his baby girl wiggle her puffy diapered bottom as she moved to him. Picking her up under her arms, Harvey stood her up and finished her look by zipping up her pinafore dress at the back and helping her slip into her ballet flats.

"How do you want your hair, little one?" Harvey asked, taking out the paci Millie didn't want to let go.

"Like this, Daddy," Millie said, running into the bathroom, coming back and taking his hand when he didn't follow her, Millie walked back into the bathroom and pushed him onto the edge of the bath, making him sit down. Harvey liked how excited Millie was, as she climbed up onto his lap before she started to do her hair in a messy ponytail.

"That's what you like?" Harvey asked Millie who had started to give his face little kisses.

"Yes, Daddy," Millie said excitedly. He had to admit; it did suit her. Her sparkling blue eyes smiled as he picked her up and carried her back into the bedroom.

"What should Daddy wear today?" Harvey asked Millie despite having no intention of actually letting her have a say in his outfit.

"Something pretty," Millie giggled making Harvey laugh despite himself. He took out his tan, Italian leather boots, thick denim, dark navy jeans, and a tight white T-shirt.

"Look, baby girl, Daddy is going to match with you," Harvey said, referring to their shirts. Next, he took his designer tan leather jacket and put it on, playfully flexing for Millie who just laughed.

"Daddy, you're so silly," she laughed as Harvey opened his arms wide and scooped Millie up in huge bear hug.

"I love you, Millie," Harvey said before realizing the words had escaped. Millie looked up at him, touching his face, her eyes melting his heart and her cheeky smile, making him beam.

"I love you too Harvey," Millie said, taking the moment he had given them. Staying in that space, he kissed her passionately using his tongue to part her lips, wanting to devour her. Millie, wanting to go back to her little space, playfully pushed him off her.

"Daddy!" She squealed, making Harvey laugh and bend his head.

"What can I say, princess, you're just so tempting," he said, taking her hand deciding that it was time to go before he ravaged her again, unsure of how her body would cope.

Chapter 9

"I thought you said we were going to brunch, Daddy?" Millie asked as Harvey who was happily singing along to a country song that played on the radio. Millie looked out the window and saw the tree-lined gravel track they were driving along. Finishing his song, Harvey turned the radio down and looked at Millie. Placing a hand up her skirt, he carelessly groped her diapered pussy, groaning in frustration as he remembered how she took him so obediently.

"We are going for brunch. Brunch with a friend of Daddy's. He lives just up here," Harvey said, lifting the skirt of her pinafore and taking her hands to hold it back for him.

"Yeah, good girl," Harvey said sincerely as he stroked and cupped her roughly. Driving into a clearing, Millie saw the shed looking building and was surprised when she saw the ogre looking man walk from the front.

"He's your friend?" Millie said shocked that Harvey would know someone so different to him. The man was roughly the same build, but instead of muscle, he just had mass. His head was shaved, and he had tattoos on both his hands. He wore a baggy black T-shirt and loose fitting blue washed jeans and big chunky work boots.

"Kept your skirt up," Harvey said, narrowing his eyes on Millie as she began to cover herself. Surprised, Millie lifted her skirt again just as the man appeared at the window and looked straight onto her pussy. He opened Millie's door and blocked her way, smiling down at her. *At least he has nice teeth and smells good*, Millie thought realising that he couldn't be poor by how white and polished his teeth were and the expensive smell of his cologne.

"Well well, what do we have here," the man teased bopping Millie on the tip of her nose before looking over at Harvey.

"Hey man," Harvey said, getting out the car and coming around to shake his hand.

"This is Millie; she's a cutie, isn't she?" Harvey said, taking Millie from the car and holding her in his arms. Millie buried her face into Harvey's chest and peeped out at the man.

"Millie, this is Uncle Ben, he is a friend of Daddy," Harvey said, patting her bottom as he walked her inside.

"She's a shy little one," Ben said, brushing her cheek with his thumb.

"Bring her over here, I've got some new toys," Ben said to Harvey as they entered his house. Millie's tummy grumbled, making both the robust men laugh.

"Maybe we fill her up first," Ben said, walking in the opposite direction. Millie hoped he meant brunch, whenever Harvey spoke like that he fucked her to exhaustion and Millie wasn't sure how she felt with the idea of letting this big ogre with his big sausage fingers plow her.

"There you go," Harvey said, placing Millie

down in an adult-sized high-chair and securing her in place with a belt around her waist and between her thighs. Millie looked shocked as Harvey left her to go into the fridge and begin to help Ben prepare brunch.

"There's a bottle warmer over there, I moved it," Ben said plainly as Harvey took a bottle of cold milk from the fridge.

"You'll have a bottle today little girl; Mama isn't here to push her big nipple into your mouth. Although, I heard she started to lactate so you might be lucky if you see her again," Harvey laughed. Ben looked at him with a curious expression.

"Willow," was all Harvey had to say before Ben was laughing.

"Yeah I heard she's come over to our side in a big way," Ben said, placing strips of bacon in a saucepan and frying eggs in another one.

"Yeah, well. Imagine my surprise when I come home and there she is, with my little angel's lips pressed to her huge jugs," Harvey said. Millie hadn't heard him speak like that before and she smirked as she remembered how much she had enjoyed it.

"Here sweetheart," Ben said offering Millie a small piece of bacon he blew on to cool down.

"Thank you, Uncle Ben," Millie said politely. Ben smirked.

"Cute, kid," Ben said, patting her on the head. Harvey beamed at her, and she liked that she made him happy.

"Open wide, little one," he said coming over with the bottle he had been warming. Millie took the bottle in both her hands and began drinking.

"She's a good girl," Harvey said, kissing her cheek and going back into the kitchen to sit at the large stone table where Ben had set up their meal. He sat down to a large wooden plate full of bacon, eggs, tomato, and home-made bread that was still warm. Millie couldn't hear them talking and finishing her bottle, she grew bored and wanted to explore. Trying to open the locked belt holding her down, she fiddled with it, getting caught by Ben who had walked back over to her.

"Oh, you want to get down? Say the magic words little girl," Ben said, reaching out to place his big hands on the lock, pushing into her diaper as he waited.

"Please, Uncle Ben," Millie said, hoping that she had got it right. Ben just laughed and shook his head.

"No, how about, I want your cock, Uncle Ben," he said, Millie's mouth gaped open.

"Oh, do you want my cock in your mouth, are you opening it for me?" Ben teased, making Millie shut her mouth quickly. Ben just laughed as he unlocked her harness and took her down. He took his time picking her up, deciding that he wanted her facing him as he carried her. Placing one hand on her back, he pushed her tits into his broad chest as his other hand reached around Millie's ass and between her thighs, pressing his hand into her diaper and against her pussy.

"Safe and sound. I could just slip my cock into you in this position. You'd better stop moving or I might just," Ben said, dropping Millie slightly and pushing the hardening bulge in his pants against her diaper covered pussy.

"Do you feel that pretty baby, that's a big toy for you to play with," Ben teased, rubbing Millie's diaper over his groin. Millie wiggled in his arms, wanting to get down as he carried her back into the room where Harvey was finishing his coffee.

"She's a little squirmer, Daddy," Ben said, placing Millie on Harvey's lap, watching as she settled straight away.

"Did she use the magic words?" Harvey asked suddenly cuffing Millie's wrists behind her back and turning her around to face Ben. Ben pushed his hips forward, enjoying how close Millie's lips were to the thick prick he wasn't even trying to hide.

"You won't need your hands for a while," Harvey said as Millie tried to struggle free. Ben just sat back down and enjoyed watching Millie's tits bounce and shake as Harvey began to bounce her on his lap.

"You lucky bastard," Ben playfully said reaching forward and slapping Millie's tits a few times predatorily. He stood up and went to the kitchen, slicing a piece of bread and drizzling honey over the top. Coming back, Harvey placed one arm around her waist and the other on the front of her chest, holding her jaw open.

"Don't fight Daddy," Harvey said, waiting until Millie stopped moving on his lap. He liked how her resistance hardened his cock, knowing that it would be resting inside her shortly. Millie ate the bread Ben fed her, breaking off small pieces and waiting for her first to swallow before he fed her the next mouthful. Beginning to feel full, Millie shook her head to the last three bit of the large piece of bread.

"Time for a little rest pretty baby," Ben said gesturing for Harvey to follow him down to the other side of the property. Millie could feel her pussy getting wet at the game they were playing, knowing that at some point, she would have two cocks dominating her bound body.

"Put her in here," Ben said, opening the door to a nursery. Millie's eyes grew wide seeing the setup. There was a large adult sized crib with soft sheets printed with fairies. A toy-box overflowing with stuffies was in the corner, and a changing table that was stocked with diapers, creams and lotions, and a box of pacifiers was placed against the wall. Millie saw that it had restraints like the high-chair had and as Harvey carried her to the crib, she giggled in delight.

"Thank you, Daddy," Millie whispered before Harvey placed a blue paci in her mouth. He smiled lovingly as he took her wrists and gently secured the locks around the silk ties.

"I can't have you escaping can I, baby girl?" Harvey said. Millie just shook her head before watching Harvey leave the room. He shut the door behind him, and Millie was surprised at how dark the room was as she closed her eyes and drifted off to sleep.

Waking up, Millie was still in darkness, but she knew that someone else was in the room with her.

"I was wondering when you'd wake up, little girl," she heard coming from behind the crib. She knew it was Ben. She hoped that Harvey knew he was in here and that it wasn't going to be another Willow incident.

"Daddy," Millie said, pushing her paci out with her tongue.

"No, Daddy's in the living room, I'm just coming in here to get you," Ben said, opening the black-out curtains to let the moonlight stream in.

"Night-time?" Millie asked, making Ben laugh.

"Yeah, little girl, night-time. You had a big sleep; we didn't you'd be out for so long," Ben said, unlocking her wrists and picking up her paci before wrapping her in a blanket and picking her up. This time Millie didn't fight his touch. He held her with one arm between her thighs, pushing her diaper into her pussy and let her legs dangle as his other arm held her around her waist and supported her head.

"Look at what sleepy girl I found," Ben said, carrying Millie into the living room, Harvey was indeed sitting in. He had been drinking, Millie could tell by the shared bottle of whiskey on the wooden table between the high-backed chairs they had been sitting in.

"There's my little girl. Put her on the floor; she can play down there while we finish this," Harvey said, pouring Ben another drink before filling his glass. A fire roared in the considerable stone fire-place, and Millie began to feel hot in her stockings as the warmth from the fire filled the air.

"Daddy, I'm hot," Millie said, crawling over to him and resting her head on his lap.

"Then let me take this off," Harvey said, taking her pinafore and stockings off leaving her in her exposed diaper and T-shirt. Ben and Harvey watched her as she played in front of them, making the stuffies that Ben had placed on the floor talk to each other and bending forward to reach the blocks that were out of reach for her stuffie castle.

"Baby, time to go home, today lasted a lot longer than I had planned," Harvey said, making Ben laugh. Millie just shook her head no, making Harvey raise an eyebrow.

"Oh, you've never said no to me before, little girl," he said, standing up and stretching. He knew he was tipsy; he could tell by how powerful he felt.

"I don't wanna go, Daddy," Millie said, continuing to play her game.

"If you don't get up, I'm going to punish you right here in front of Uncle Ben, is that what you want?" Harvey said, walking over to Millie's tower and kicking it over.

"Daddy!" Millie exclaimed, her eyes sparkling with mischief.

"Sounds like she needs a spank," Ben said, standing up and coming to stand over the top of her next to Harvey. Harvey slowly took off his belt, and Millie just turned around and wiggled her puffy bottom in his face, bending down so her face was on the floor and her ass was high in the air.

"Oh, she's asking for it," Ben laughed, slapping his friend on the back and giving him a knowing look. Harvey just nodded at him, causing Ben to smile and begin to take off his belt. Harvey struck her first, making her gasp as he brought his belt down on her padded ass.

"What? You didn't think Daddy was joking when I said that you'd be punished, did you?" Harvey said, watching as Ben belted her next. Millie just gasped as the air was belted from her lungs time after time as Harvey and Ben took it in turns to strike her. Rolling her onto her back, Harvey looked into Millie's eyes to gauge where she was at, happy when he saw her bit her bottom lip and smirk up at him.

"Get on your knees," Harvey roughly said, grabbing her hair and pulling her into position. He sat back down in his chair and watched as Millie placed her hands behind her head like he had trained her to and waited for his next instruction.

"Open your mouth," he said, watching Ben

kick off his shoes and pull his cock out. He was hairier than Harvey, liking how his caveman body looked against the women he fucked. Pulling on his dick as he eyed Millie's obedient and vulnerable position, Ben moved into her line of sight, making Millie gasp as she saw his protruding cock pushing through his fist.

"Yeah, exactly," Ben said as he pushed his cock into Millie's mouth until her face was pressed against his dense black fur, burying her nose in his thick patch of black pubic hair.

"Why you fighting?" Ben said, holding her mouth firmly onto him as he felt his cock jerk in excitement in her mouth. Pulling out slowly, he liked the long string of saliva that connected his cock to her mouth before thrusting back into her making it spurt over her face, wetting his furry balls as he forced her to gobble his cock.

"She's a good girl," Ben said, pulling back out, slapping his cock against Millie's face, pushing the tip into her cheek. Harvey had come to sit behind her, taking off her diaper as Ben turkey slapped her until her face was covered with spit and pre-cum.

"You won't need that anymore," Harvey laughed, feeling how heavy Millie had made her diaper. He took a wet wipe and wiped her clean, happy she was such a good girl for wetting her diaper. He walked over to the bin and threw the used diaper and wipes in before coming back to see that Ben was still busy filling her mouth.

"Suck my balls baby," Ben said, jerking his cock as he lowered his hairy, soft sack into her mouth.

"I said take it," Ben growled, slapping Millie's face as she struggled to fit him in her mouth. She sucked deeply, feeling him grab the back of her head and grind himself further down her throat.

"Yeah, there it is. Good girl," Ben said spilling cum from his big mushroomed tip cock onto his hand. Harvey came back behind her and spat on his hand before roughly rubbing it over her pussy.

"Here's, Daddy," he said, shoving his pulsing cock into Millie's cunt without warning making her scream around Ben's balls, making them vibrate just exciting him more.

"Oh, dude, make her scream again," Ben said, pumping his cock faster and closing his eyes. Harvey just laughed and sucked a butt plug before stuffing her ass. Ben reached down and grabbed at Millie's tits as she screamed again, her throat vibrating against Ben's balls as he came.

"Get her up here," Harvey said, holding her thighs open and lifting her as he stood. Pulling his balls from Millie's mouth, she was surprised they had filled as their size had grown, filling out and looking like a big furry marshmallow. Harvey carried her to the chair he had been previously sitting in and sat her down on his lap, her face towards him resting on his chest.

"Watch this. Bounce for Daddy," Harvey said as Millie immediately began twerking on his lap, her ass wobbling hard, shaking down on his lap as she fucked herself. Ben came behind her and slowly took out the toy that had stretched her ass. Slowly taking it from her, he liked that her ass gaped, looking ready to be filled again.

"Do you think she can take this monster?" Ben said, rubbing his big mushroom tip against her asshole.

"Yeah, stick it in dude, enjoy her," Harvey said, reaching around and spreading Millie's asshole further. Ben smirked as he stuffed the tip in, feeling Millie, try and close herself.

"Your Daddy said I could have you baby girl, and that's what I'm going to do, I'm going to empty all the cream you just filled my balls within this ass," Ben said grabbing Millie's hair in his fist as his other hand held her down by her shoulder as he speared her ass until he was balls deep inside her just as Harvey thrust into her filling her pussy, both men cumming in her at the same time. Millie squealed as they began fucking her again, their cum spilling from her holes as she was taken by the two large men, being entirely overpowered by their embrace.

"Where do you think you are going?" Harvey said as Millie wriggled on his lap.

"I told you that you'd be punished didn't I sweetheart," he added, picking her up and pulling his cock from her, making her squirt all over the floor. Ben laughed as his cock made a popping sound as his tip pulled from her ass. Harvey put her down in the cummy mess they had made as Millie's holes oozed cum on the cold, slate floor Harvey had laid her on.

"I don't think there's much use continuing, she's all used up for tonight," he said walking to the kitchen and taking out two beers and opening them on the side of the bench before stepping back, his still erect cock swinging as he walked.

"Cheers," Ben said toasting as he stood on one side of Millie and Harvey standing on the other side.

"Knock knock mother fuckers, I got your text," Millie heard Willow announce as she walked into the room, stopping when she saw Millie laying on the floor.

"What did you do to my little one!?" Willow exclaimed making Millie burst into tears. She had been happy so far, but something about Willow just made her feel so nervous and more uncomfortable than getting fucked as she had just been fuck did.

"Look, you made her cry," Harvey teased, pouring some of his beer over Millie's face.

"Oh baby girl, come to Mama," Willow said, pushing Harvey away who just laugh before sighing in contented bliss and falling back into his chair.

"Say bye bye to Millie, Teddy," Harvey mocked, shaking his cock at Millie as Willow bent down and took her hand, walking her out of the room.

"She's great, hey? Such a slut," Harvey said, finishing his beer in one chug.

"Yeah dude, and you said she is an accounted? It's always the quiet ones, isn't it?" Ben said, remembering how good it had felt to use Millie.

"Why did you text Willow?" Ben asked, making Harvey laugh.

"That's my little psychological treat for her. She tries to tell me she's straight, but Willow got her good," Harvey said impressed with himself.

Willow had taken Millie to Ben's shower and washed her clean, making sure to soap her gently. The markings from Harvey and Ben's belts visible despite Millie having had her diaper to protect her ass.

"You must have been such a bad girl to be punished like this little one," Willow said, taking Millie's hand and leading her out of the bath.

"I just said no to Daddy," Millie said, her little voice escaping as she fell back into her small headspace, with Willow being so gentle and loving with her.

"Well, that'll do it," Willow laughed before kissing Millie's cheek.

"But it's ok because Mama is here now and you're always safe with Mama, aren't you?" Willow said. She liked that Millie was so inexperienced with women and just blushed and fought herself over wanting what was happening to her.

"Say it little one," Willow said, catching Millie off guard, not understanding what Willow wanted.

"Say, you are safe with Mama," Willow said, helping Millie understand. Millie burned red and bit her bottom lip, squirming nervously in Willow's hands, and she held the towel still and looked expectantly into Millie's eyes.

"I'm safe with Mama," Millie almost whispered, looking down but not getting further than Willow's big sweater covered tits.

"Soon, little girl," Willow said, catching Millie staring. Millie looked up ready to try and say she wasn't looking, but Willow just raised her eyebrow, and Millie stopped.

"Don't even try to pretend you don't want them. Mama even has a special treat for you," Willow said making Millie remember that Harvey had said Willow had milk now.

"But first, let's get you dressed and all ready for bed. You've had a big day," Willow said, taking Millie into the nursery and laying her on the changing table. Willow selected a purple diaper and added extra padding, knowing Millie's pussy would be leaking her captures cum for hours to come. Patting Millie as she fastened the sticky tabs down firmly securing the diaper in place.

"Are you going to be Mama's little bunny tonight, sweetheart?" Willow asked, taking out a white fluffy bunny onesie and dressing Millie before she had responded.

"Why am I asking? You'll do everything Mama wants because if you think they punished you, oh little lady, you've never felt Mama's wrath," Willow said putting a white paci in Millie's mouth before helping her down and pushing her to the floor.

"Crawl to Mama, little one," Willow said, walking over to the big rocking chair in the opposite corner and sitting down. She placed Millie on her la, and Millie knew what was going to come next.

"Is this what you want little one?" Willow whispered as she lifted her sweater off her head and pulled out her breast from its cup.

"I'm not really," Millie began to say making Willow rolled her eyes.

"Yeah, I know you're not really into girls, blah blah blah, shut up, baby and suck Mama's milky tits like a good girl," Willow said placing her nipple in Millie's mouth and squeezing her tits making her milk squirt into Millie's mouth.

"Yummy isn't it, little one?" Willow asked, already knowing the answer, watching Millie close her eyes and melt into her arms as she nursed. Millie made soft slurping noises making Willow smile and stroke her cheek as she nursed Millie, her limp body soft and warm in her arms.

"I was wondering how long it would take for you to appear," Willow said seeing Harvey walk into the nursery. He had showered and was wearing comfortable house clothes as he came and stood by Willow's side, bending down to kiss her on the cheek.

"Thanks," he said, referring to the gentle aftercare she was giving Millie.

"How could I say no to this little one?" Willow said making Millie open her eyes.

"Daddy!" She exclaimed happily before going back to suckling on Willow's massive tits as she looked up at him.

"Hey there little one, is Mama looking after you?" Harvey said going over to taking a blanket from the crib and wrapping it over Willow's shoulders.

"Thank you, Daddy," Willow sensually teased.

"I still think we should play happy families, look how much little Millie needs a Mama," Willow said stroking Millie's hair out of her face while rocking her in her arms.

"And look at how much Teddy needs to be kept entertained. Our little girl can't do that job all by herself, we both know that" Willow said grabbing Harvey's cock, feeling it harden immediately as she stroked him.

"I'll think about it," he said in a hoarse throat making Millie laugh.

"What are you laughing at hey," Harvey said, kissing her forehead.

"You, Daddy. Why are you pretending you don't love Mama," Millie asked around Willow's nipple, milk spilling from her mouth and down her cheek.

"Yeah, Daddy, why do you pretend you don't love me?" Willow asked more serious than Harvey was prepared for. He walked over to the changing table and took a wet-wipe before passing it to Willow and deeply thinking about the proposal.

"What would that even look like?" He asked coming to sit in front of Willow on the floor, crossing his legs and beginning to rub her feet.

"I could get used to this," Willow said, bouncing Millie gently as Harvey massaged her heels.

"I guess our little one would go to work

Monday-Friday, see her friends on the weekend. Be our baby every night, and when you've destroyed her, Mama can come and look after her before she goes and finishes you off. I would move my stuff back into your house; Millie would move in too. You'd still work like you do, so would I, we could go on family night at the cinemas. It'd be hot, as long as everyone remembered that Millie doesn't like girls," Willow said, teasing her and making her giggle. Harvey began massaging her other foot, and Willow swapped Millie onto her other breast.

"What do you think, baby?" Harvey asked Millie.

"Do you want Mama all the time?" He added but already knowing the answer by Millie's excitedly giggles and nodding head.

"Yes please, Daddy," she said her hands coming up to play with Willow's tits.

"Right then. I guess we can give it a go and see how it works for a month or so," Harvey said surprised at how his life had turned upside down by the two women in front of him. He thought back to how simple life had been before Willow and Millie but quickly decided that what he had now was far better.

Chapter 10

Harvey watched as the two women began to over-run his house, finding it strange that he enjoyed them and their noise, their make-up covering his bathroom counter and their constant giggling. They had all seamlessly meshed their lives together, surprising him at just how easy it had been. He had heard the stories of people who had tried to do this, and it had all ended terribly. With one person feeling left out or jealousy rearing its ugly head and yet here they all were, eating breakfast on a Saturday morning after a week of work and meetings.

"Pass Mama the milk, baby girl," Willow said to Millie who had been given her coloring in book after she finished her fruit platter first. Millie held a fist full of pens in one hand, as she reached for the jug, just for Harvey to place his hand on it first.

"She's too little to lift it, Will," Harvey said causing Willow to raise her eyebrow over her reading glasses.

"Too little to follow Mama's direction, I don't think so," Willow said taking Millie's chin in her hand and shaking her head slightly before accepting the jug from Harvey. Harvey just laughed.

"She was last night," he said remembering how they had both fucked Millie until she couldn't stand without her legs buckling and when Willow had tried to make her, she had to catch Millie every time she tried.

"Well yes, she was," Willow said, standing up and kissing Millie gently on her lips before looking down at her drawing.

"Are you drawing a cute picture for Mama?" Willow asked, letting her hand casually grope Millie's tits over the top of the fluffy yellow sweater Harvey had dressed her in. Millie just giggled and squirmed as she was felt causing

Willow to lick her lips at Harvey playfully before going into the kitchen.

"I'm going for a run, did you have any plans today?" Willow asked coming back with a sippy cup with water for Millie and a coffee for Harvey. He waited for her to place it in front of him before playfully grabbing her hips and pulling her onto his lap, making her laugh.

"You fool," Willow laugh slapping his chest but settling on his lap gently rocking her hips, enjoying how she felt him between her thighs.

"No, we do need to get the last of Millie's things from her house though. Maybe we can go to dinner after we do that?" Harvey suggested before getting kissed passionately, Millie looking up beaming at how lustful they were for each other. She loved having both of their affection and had found it interesting that she wasn't jealous of Willow. *Maybe it's coz I'm their baby as if I'd get jealous of Mama;* she thought to herself watching as Willow slipped her tongue into Harvey's mouth and sucked it sensually.

"Sounds good to me. See you soon, baby," Willow said, getting up as she copped a firm slap on her ass from Harvey and grabbed Millie's hand as she tried to slap her ass as well.

"Oh cheeky baby," Willow said, flicking her hand away and making Millie giggle as she sucked her paci and continued to color.

"Let's tidy up while Mama is gone baby girl," Harvey said as Millie started to become fussy. She had been kept in her high-chair for the last hour, and Harvey knew that she needed to get down soon. He carefully unlocked her, feeling her between her thighs as he placed her down on the floor.

"Stay there," he said suddenly, his voice desperate with lust. Millie watched as he disappeared, just to return with a thick vibrator and chastity belt.

"Oh, no, Daddy. I don't wanna," Millie said, trying to slap his big hands away.

"Shh little one, Daddy doesn't care what you want. This is what I want, so it's happening,"

Harvey said, lubing the toy with his spit and pinning Millie down with his thigh while the other held her legs apart.

"Daddy likes his little girl filled; you know that don't pretend you don't like it," Harvey plainly said pulling the top of Millie's diaper down and stuffing her with the toy making her squeal as it forced its a way inside her. Turning it on, Harvey watched as Millie's nipples went hard under her sweater. He had denied her ever to wear a bra in the house and liked the easy access she was forced to accept as he held one hand to her pussy holding the toy in place and reached under her sweater to flick and tease her nipples.

"Daddy likes you ready to be fucked," Harvey said, taking the belt and effortlessly pulling it up Millie's thighs as she felt her pussy start to relax around the toy inside of her. He locked it in place as a wicked smile spread across his lips.

"Tell Daddy which hole is still free to be fucked," Harvey whispered in Millie's ear as he placed her on his lap and bent her forward.

"My ass, Daddy," Millie said, worried that he would try and fuck her there next.

"That's right little one, remember that. That if you are a naughty girl for Daddy, that's where my cock is going to go and stay for a while when we watch cartoons later," Harvey said grabbing her hips and roughly dry humping her ass making himself hard. Standing up, he just laughed as Millie whimpered and stayed on the floor as he began to tidy up from breakfast, his cock hard in his grey sweat pants.

"Did you turn Daddy on again little girl?" Willow said coming back from changing into her work out gear. She walked over to where Millie was standing and raised an eyebrow as she saw her baby belted and horny.

"We were just playing, weren't we Millie?" Harvey teased, jerking his cock. Willow came to sit next to Millie on the floor and swooned as Millie crawled to her, resting her face in Willow's deep cleavage, her sports bra making the top of her tits push out of her singlet.

"I know what you want baby girl, but Mama likes you like this too so you'll have to be a good girl and stay like that until I get back. Here," Willow said, pulling her tit out and pushing Millie's mouth to her nipple. Millie grabbed Willow with both hands and suckled greedily, feeling the vibrator buried in her cunt make her clit throb. Willow held Millie's face close and pulled her into her arms as she nursed, waiting until Millie had settled and closed her eyes before gently taking her off.

"Be a good girl for Daddy, Mama will be back soon," Willow said lovingly to Millie who just nodded her head as Willow pushed her paci back in her mouth.

"Have fun," Willow called knowingly as she closed the door behind her.

Harvey had indeed had his fun with Millie before Willow had come back. They had painted, made cookies and Millie had helped with the washing before Harvey had taken her to the nursey they had all made and tied Millie to the wall.

"You aren't being punished little girl; Daddy just wants to make sure that you don't go anywhere while I work. Here, have your toys and be a good girl," Harvey said as he placed Millie's favorite stuffies in front of her and watched as she began to play.

Harvey walked down the hallway and into his room, lay on his bed, and sighed. He had never thought his life would turn out like this. *Having two women to fuck at my command, given I always have to ask Willow first, but she never says no, and Millie*, he thought reaching down to touch himself. She had been the perfect baby. Easy to train, easy to please, always willingly and so beautiful. Willow had dyed the tips of Millie's blonde hair purple, and it matched her deep blue eyes perfectly. Her skinny frame making him crave to touch her on sight, and he loved how open she had been to all his suggestions. *Is this just life now? This perfect fucking life with these two amazing women. I'm one lucky bastard*; he laughed to himself as Willow stormed into the room.

"Hey," Harvey said startled to be interrupted.

"Why is my little girl chained to the wall?" Willow said stripping, her body sweaty from her run, her hair messy like she'd just been fucked.

"I just needed a minute and didn't want her to run away," Harvey said, standing up and walking to Willow who placed her hand on his chest.

"Down boy, Mama isn't in the mood," Willow said, taking Harvey by surprise.

"If you were my little one I'd make you take a pounding for that," Harvey said, grabbing her hips and grinding his bulge into her pussy.

"But I'm not am I?" Willow teased, laying on the floor and beginning to play with herself. Harvey sat at the edge of his bed and shamelessly began jerking himself off at the sight of the powerful women fucking her pussy.

"I have an idea for Millie," Willow said breathlessly as she slid a finger into her cunt, gasping as it reached her hilt. Harvey knew what she was feeling, his cock had felt it countless times, and he closed his eyes, remembering how tight she was there.

"Yeah, what?" He groaned as he felt his orgasm building.

"I can't tell you," Willow said, making Harvey frown.

"Why not?" He almost yelled, standing up as he pumped his cock.

"Because your cock is about to be in my mouth," Willow said, opening her mouth and sticking out her tongue. Harvey excitedly straddled her face, pushing his cock down her throat and feeling her gag around his tip as he shot into her.

"Fuck yeah," Harvey groaned as he pumped Willow's mouth with his load shuddering as she swallowed him deeply.

"Finish me," Willow said when Harvey finally pulled his cock from her throat. He just laughed as he went to his cupboard and took out a paddle before leaving the room.

"Son of a bitch," Willow said, laying her head down on the floor and played with herself again, closing her eyes only to open them again as Harvey came back into the room.

"Baby," Willow said in surprise, reaching out to Millie who still had her diaper on.

"You're going to play with Mama until she's happy, baby girl," Harvey instructed unlocking her belt and reaching into her diaper. He roughly pulled the toy from Millie's pussy, making her squeal which just made Willow rub her clit harder.

"Come to Mama, baby girl," Willow said lovingly. Harvey reached her first, shoving the wet toy into her cunt and making Willow arch her back as the intruder made her cum instantly. She grabbed Millie's hand and held her back as her orgasm ravaged through her.

"No, baby," Willow said, making Millie confused. Willow let her climax die back down before she spoke again. Harvey had ripped Millie's diaper off and was busy slamming into her pussy as Willow held her wrist to the floor.

"Bring her here," Willow said breathlessly as Harvey reached down to pin Millie's head on the floor as he emptied inside of her. When he was finished, Millie got up and crawled to where Willow was patting her lap and wrapping her arms around Millie's younger body; Willow began nursing her as Harvey came back for more.

"Daddy's not finished," Harvey said lifting Millie's leg and fucking her as she lay cradled on her side in Willow's arms. Willow knew Millie was near her limit by the pained wincing and squeaks she was making around her nipple.

"Be gentle, Daddy," Willow said, eyeing him warningly as he slowed his onslaught. Millie curled her arms into her chest as Willow held her tight, forcing her to suckle as she was power fucked by Harvey.

"Red, red," Millie said suddenly, pushing Willow away as Harvey pulled out instantly, his cum spilling out onto the wooden floor.

"Millie are you ok, tell us what's going on,"

Harvey said, dropping to his knees and holding out his hand to Millie.

"It just hurt too much, I was playing, and then this and it was all just too much," Millie said as tears began to roll down her face. Willow bit her bottom lip and ran her fingers through her hair before she stood up.

"Hey come on sweetie, let's get you cleaned up and settled," she said, taking Millie into the shower. Harvey followed and watched as Willow took the lead and clean Millie's cum covered body, gently rubbing her pussy clean as Millie cuddled into her.

"I'm proud of you for saying red Millie," Harvey said lovingly as he reached out to touch her cheek. Millie just sighed as she rested her head in Harvey's hands while Willow finished washing her body.

"Thanks, Daddy. I'm happy you're not mad," Millie sleepily said.

"I could never be mad sweetheart," Harvey said as he helped Willow take Millie from the bath.

He wrapped her big pink fluffy towel around her and picked her up as he carried her to the living room.

"Where do you need to be Millie," Willow said stroking Millie's hair and offering Millie her paci. Millie just nodded her head and opened her mouth for Willow who pushed her paci past her pink lips.

"Take her to the nursery, Daddy," Willow said before going to the kitchen to heat a bottle.

"There you go little one," Harvey said, placing Millie onto the changing table and beginning to diaper her. He sprinkled fresh powder over her and rubbed it in gently before seeing Willow return with Millie's blankie and bottle. He closed the tabs and pulled on her safari onesie before picking her up again and taking her to the rocking chair. Sitting down, he cradled her in his arms as Willow placed the blanket on top of Millie and passed the bottle of Harvey.

"You're a good girl, next time we play we will make sure you're a big girl first, ok baby?"

Willow said, placing her hands on her hips and watching her lover.

"I'm sorry Daddy hurt you, baby," Harvey said, bringing Millie up to his lips to kiss her face gently before continuing to rock her to sleep. As her bottle emptied, and her eyes grow tired, Harvey carried her to the crib and lowered her down.

"See you in a little while baby," he said to a sleeping Millie before leaving the room and shutting the door behind him.

"Fuck," Willow said as she saw Harvey walk into the living room. Willow had finished off tidying the house and was reading a magazine while she waited for Harvey to return.

"Right!?" Harvey said, sitting down next to her. They both sat in silence and listened to the birds outside.

"I mean, we do fuck her like she's a slave," Willow said, turning to face Harvey.

"Yeah, I know. I feel so bad," Harvey said his eyes growing wide and shaking his head.

"Same. Has she ever stopped it before?" Willow asked.

"No never, usually I catch her before she goes over the edge but, not this time," Harvey said, annoyed at himself.

"What do you need?" Willow said, seeing how disappointed he was with himself. He looked up at her curiously.

"What?" He asked, unsure of what she was meaning.

"Well, we just looked after Millie, but she's not the only one who is feeling shit. Do you need to go for a walk or be reminded that you are a great man and such a loving Daddy?" Willow suggested making him laugh.

"I don't feel so great right now," he said, leaning forward and putting his hands on his knees.

"Let's look at the facts. You stopped the minute she needed to when you were like mid-orgasm. You took the time to look after her and get her back into a good space and are giving her what she needs. You're ok; she still thinks you are amazing," Willow said, placing her hand on his back.

"What about you?" Harvey asked, turning his head to look at her.

"What about me?" Willow asked, confused.

"Well, don't you feel bad too?" Harvey asked, sitting up to look at her.

"Yeah I do, but she's not the first girl who has said stop to me, in fact, I get it a lot. I have already gone through my; I don't know, Dom drops if you like and I know that everything will be fine. You've just never had a girl you like fucking so much, so you've never felt this before. But it's ok, it's all going to be ok Harvey," Willow said, hugging him.

Chapter 11

"Daddy," Millie called from the nursery a few hours later. Harvey hadn't realized that he had fallen asleep until Millie's voice calling his name woke him. Getting up, he hurried to her side only to see her smiling up at him.

"Hi, there sweetie, did you have a good nap?" Harvey said, picking her out of the crib and holding her in his arms. Millie just nodded as she snuggled into him and felt his heart beat against her face.

"Daddy, can we go out like we did before," Millie said as Harvey walked her into the kitchen and made her lunch.

"Like, when you came home from work and went to a bar before being Daddy's little diapered princess?" Harvey teased, making her blush.

"Yeah," Millie said, taking the spoon and

feeding herself the pumpkin soup Harvey had heated up for her.

"Yeah, sure. You'll still be Daddy's baby, though. Do you want to go just us or take Mama with us?" Harvey said as Willow came into the house with the last of Millie's things. She had gone out to collect the remaining three bags of Millie's clothes from her home. They had found people to rent the house out too and Millie had been excited that she'd be earning money as a landlord.

"Take Mama where?" Willow said, catching the end of the conversation.

"Nowhere, Mama," Millie said, going back to eat her soup. Harvey looked at her and hoped that their world wasn't falling around them. Willow just raised her eyebrows and continued down the hall to Harvey's room.

"Let's keep it a secret and take Mama out to something special, Daddy," Millie quickly said before Harvey could ask her if everything was alright, relieving his anxiety.

"Oh, ok that sounds like a fun idea," Harvey

said whispering with matching excitement.

"Yeah, but I want to be a big girl for that night please, Daddy?" Millie asked, making Harvey lick his lips with excitement.

"Sure thing," he said, his eyes sparkling with the curiosity of what Millie was planning.

Millie had been swamped with work all week, working well into the night from Monday to Friday. With the plan for everyone to meet at 7:30, Millie knew she would be late.

"Hello little one," Willow said, answering Harvey's phone. She was just sliding her freshly pedicured feet into her black patent heels.

"Hey, um, I might be a little late, I'll be there by eight though ok?" Millie said, making Willow laugh.

"Oh baby, are you in your big girl office working hard? Can't you call me Mama because someone might learn that you are my little princess?" Willow teased making Millie blush. She felt a shiver run through her body as she heard

Harvey in the background.

"Hey, baby, you on your way?" Harvey said, taking the phone off Willow.

"I just told, um, Willow, that I'll be like 30mins late. I just really need to get this stuff sorted," Millie said. Harvey paused before he spoke again.

"I don't know who you are talking about. Is it Mama?" Harvey said, the smile he tried to suppress spreading across his face and escaping his voice.

"Don't," Millie said with a warning in her voice.

"Or what baby? You'll tell Daddy off?" Harvey said, enjoying the discomfort he was putting Millie in.

"Say it. Say, Daddy; I'm going to be late," Harvey said aggressively. Millie held her breath and swallowed hard. Looking around the office, Millie saw one or two colleagues still typing on their computers and bit her bottom lip.

"I know you think you're a big girl, but

you're still mine, and I've told you what I expect," Harvey said, sitting down on the couch. Willow came to sit beside him and placed her hands on his lap, resting against his large muscular body.

"I can't," Millie said, begging to be let off this once. Harvey put her on speaker and stared at Willow excitedly.

"We are waiting for you little one," Willow teased, both laughing as Millie groaned down the phone.

"I'll be late, Daddy," Millie said quietly, bending down to speak under her desk.

"What about Mama, you were rude to her as well," Harvey said zipping up Willow's black dress.

"Mama, I'm sorry," Millie said, her voice breaking and her little voice escaping. Millie burned red as she sat back up, hoping that no one had heard her.

"You don't even know how sorry you're going to be," Harvey said, taking the phone and ending the call before Millie could reply.

"Too harsh?" Harvey asked Willow who was pouring herself a red wine.

"No, fuck her, the rude little bitch," Willow said, her heels sounding loudly against the slate floors.

"Oh, we will," Harvey said, offering his hand to her as they headed to the door.

Millie knew she was fucked. Mostly because it was 8:45 by the time she reached the bar, and Harvey's promise to punish her loomed over her head. Walking into the bar, Millie smiled as the smell of beer hit her. She took off her coat and placed it on the hook by the door as she let her eyes wander. The room was dark, men in suits drank the week's problems away, and she watched as they drank scotch straight. Smelling the familiar smell of Harvey's cologne, Millie turned around smiling.

"Hi Daddy," she said upon seeing him. He had dressed in his signature heavy dark denim jeans. His slight pink oxford button down had the sleeves rolled up. *Only a very tough man can pull that off*, Millie thought as he held her like she was the most precious thing in the world. He had got his lines and fade away touched up, and he had worn his large platinum ring on the middle finger of his left hand and his watch on his right wrist. Releasing Millie from the bear hug he had held her in, he took in her appearance, enjoying that she had made sure her make-up was fresh. Her black, high-waisted business skirt was tucked into her emerald green lace blouse. Harvey could see that she had worn her black lace bra underneath and had taken the black singlet that he had handed her that morning off. Her hair tumbled down both sides of her face, and her baby blues stared at him with all the innocence in the world.

"See something you like, Daddy?" Millie teased, pushing into him as she passed and went to greet Willow.

"Someone was a naughty girl," Willow whispered in Millie's ear as she held her, biting her ear roughly until Millie pulled away in pain.

"I'm sorry, Mama," Millie tried to say but

had Willow's hand covering her mouth before she could finish.

"Did I say I fucking wanted to hear your reasons for being a disrespectful little bitch?" Willow said, sitting back on the bar lounge and crossed her long legs, flicking her foot up and down as her eyes burned holes into Millie.

"I should have you down on your fucking knees right here begging for my forgiveness," Willow said as she slid her glass along the table.

"Get me a drink, that'll be a good start," Willow added, staring at Millie. Millie got up, taking the glass in her hand before walking to the bar where Harvey was waiting.

"So, that went well, I'm assuming?" He laughed, taking a sip of his beer. Millie just looked at him with her big puppy dog eyes.

"Don't look at me like that, baby, you did it to yourself," he said, paying for the drinks and walking back to where Willow was sitting.

"How was your day?" Millie asked Harvey as he sat with his arm around her and Willow.

Willow had placed her hand on his thigh and was slowing stroking him while she drank.

"Just the usual. A guy that I've been training for three years finally reached his goal weight, so that was awesome," Harvey replied, kissing the top of her forehead. Millie rested her head on Harvey's shoulder and sighed, the stress of the week finally lifting.

"Have you finished what you've been working on?" Willow asked, reaching her hand over to stroke Millie's cheek affectionately, her eyes softening as she felt Millie's soft skin.

"Yeah, finally. It was so crazy; everything just seemed to happen all at once. It's never been that busy before. But it's all sorted now so thank goodness," Millie explained sipping her drink slowly. Harvey held the glass to her lips and tipped the rest of it down her throat.

"Come on, let's get out of here," he said, smiling knowingly at Willow. Millie was confused; she had planned for them to stay for at least a few drinks.

"Well, since we had so much time to kill while we waited for you, we've come up with a new plan," Harvey said taking Millie's hand and pulling her through the crowd of people who were now standing around the bar. He grabbed her coat and pulled her outside into the cold air of the night, making Millie's head feel dizzy. Harvey whistled for a taxi as Willow helped Millie put on her coat and wrapped her arm around her predatorily.

"Where to Sir?" The taxi driver asked as Harvey got in the car. Willow pushed Millie into the back seat and pulled her to her side as the car drove away.

"72 on Blackwood thanks," Harvey said smiling down into his lap.

"Mama, where are we going?" Millie asked. Willow was busy groping her tits underneath her coat before she bent her head and kissed Millie passionately.

"Don't ask questions slut," Willow whispered into the kiss, making Millie's eyes go wide with fearful anticipation.

The taxi driver pulled into an abandoned stockyard and Harvey tipped him generously and told him to be back there in four hours. Nodding, the man took the cash and drove away, leaving the three of them standing by the lamp post light.

"Well, you've been a bad girl Millie, and do you know what happens to bad girls?" Harvey said, grabbing her by her chin and shaking her head.

"No, Daddy," Millie said swallowing hard.

"You don't? You're not that stupid, think," Harvey grabbing a handful of her hair and dragging her behind him, making her stumble on her heels as he walked her to the door of a tall building.

"They get punished," Millie said softly, wincing as Willow slapped her ass.

"They get punished, Daddy," Willow corrected.

"Maybe we've been too nice to you little one, maybe you have forgotten that your ours and that you promised to be a good girl and follow our rules. Maybe we need to teach you a lesson," Willow said, continuing to spank Millie as she tried to escape Harvey's grip.

"Don't you fucking dare move," he instructed, holding Millie's throat in his other hand and gripped her firmly until she took the spanking Willow was giving her silently.

"Good girl," Willow hissed as Millie began to whine with each spank. Harvey opened the door to the warehouse and turned the light on, taking Millie and pushing her inside. Stumbling, she fell on her hands and knees but looked up to take in the room.

"Daddy, what is this place?" Millie asked, making Willow roll her eyes.

"Shut up," she aggressively said, pushing a ball gag into Millie's mouth and securing it before Millie could resist.

"Uncle Ben is in the, let's just say, import and export business. He said we could use his playroom tonight," Harvey said, picking Millie up and taking her to a flogging cross. Pressing her body quickly to the cross, he and Willow secured her wrists above her head and her ankles apart, before standing back to take in their handy work. Millie struggled against her restraints, only adding to their amusement. He ran his fingertips over her body, enjoying that her back was to them and that she couldn't see what was going to happen to her.

"Do you think you can escape?" Harvey whispered in her ear as he took the hem of her skirt and ripped it in half, pulling the ruined material off her body and exposing her bare ass.

"Oh you are a little slut," Willow said, suddenly bringing a leather whip down onto Millie's ass. Millie just gasped as Willow began her assault, only stopping to spank Millie with both her hands.

"You better not ever fucking forget my name again, do you understand me?!" Willow growled into Millie's ear before going back to whip her. Harvey had poured himself a whiskey and was sitting on a chair as he watched and waited.

"I think you missed a spot," he said when

Willow was finished. Standing up, Millie could hear his unmistakable foot-steps coming up behind her and grew wet with excitement. Placing one hand on the back of Millie's neck, he brought his full hand down on the top of her thighs making her squeal in pain as his handprint left significant red marks on her soft skin.

"Oh, it appears I did, good thing Daddy is here, isn't it princess," Willow mocked as she took a tube of lube and squirted it into her hands. She knew Millie would be wet, but she also knew she wanted to fuck her raw tonight and began to rub her hard, sliding her fingers in without warning and fucked her roughly.

"She'll take it," Willow said to Harvey who kicked his boots off followed by his shirt. He walked behind the cross to look at Millie in her eyes and cupped her face with his hands, rubbing her cheeks with his thumbs lovingly as Millie felt something slide up and down her slit. Her eyes going wide, with fear as she saw Willow come to stand next to Harvey.

"Who could it be baby?" Harvey said as he and Willow walked back around behind her and out of sight as the unknown man spread her open and shoved himself inside her. Groaning in relief as his dick grew inside her, he held her hips as he pulled himself out of her tight cunt. He liked that there was no other choice for her than to take his long slow strokes, feeling his balls fill and become full, squishing against her ass as he filled her again slowly, and holding himself inside of her, making her feel him.

"Bye baby, have fun," Harvey was suddenly saying in her ear as he patted her on the head, took Willow's hand and walked out of the room.

Chapter 12

"Yeah, oh god, yeah," Ben said as he thrust into Millie's dripping cunt. She had long since discovered who was fucking her as Ben had taken her down from the flogging cross after cumming for the second time. He had bound her to a swing, suspending her in the air and teased her, saying how Harvey had told him she liked to swing into cock as he positioned a fucking machine with a thick dildo behind her swinging her into it by gripping her hair in a fist, only keeping her still to stuff her mouth full of his soft fleshly cock and hairy balls. He held her there, getting spit roasted by the machine and his cock until she had sucked him hard again, covering her face with his cream as he came hard.

"Are you still wet, slut? Fuck I'm a good guy for giving a shit and not just fucking you raw like whores like you deserve," Ben said pulling his cock from her mouth and walking behind her, taking the machine from her pussy. He took the tube of lube and pushed the opening into her cunt, squirting carelessly, filling her with lube until it dripped from her.

"What a fucking mess," Ben said, slapping her sensitive cunt until she was wriggling away from his touch.

"Where the fuck do you think you are going, you're mine bitch, your Daddy didn't want to fuck a naughty bitch like you, so he gave you to me for the night, and we haven't even started yet," Ben said, taking a pair of scissors and holding Millie still as he began to cut her blouse and bra off.

"As if you'll need these, how am I supposed to clamp your big tits if you're all covered up trying to hide from me?" Ben said roughly grabbing her tits and pulling them down with his thick fingers, rolling her nipples between his thumb and index finger until Millie was moaning against her gag.

"Yeah I know you like that, aren't I good to you," Ben said, walking to a drawer and taking out nipple clamps with a lightweight attached to them. Millie groaned in pain as he secured them to her nipples, jiggling her tits as he laughed at her struggle.

"Just wait till you've got a cock in you, then you'll feel them," Ben teased as he stuck a finger into her pussy and made her swing forward. Taking his finger back out, he ran it around her ass before pushing it inside of her.

"I need you lubed up bitch," Ben said as Millie felt him press a butt plug inside of her.

"Cute little bunny, I can see how Harvey forgets to discipline you, look how adorable you look," Ben said ruffling the bunny tail of the butt plug before abruptly sticking his cock back inside her lubed pussy making Millie give out a high pitched moan.

"Oh I see she's still disobedient, did I not tell you to shut the fuck up bitch?" Harvey's voice pierced through the room, and he grabbed her face with both hands and made her look up at him.

"I see you're still bad, let's try and fuck the naughty out of you then shall we?" Harvey sneered, taking out Millie's gag just to replace it with his hard cock and began to fuck her face.

"Well, I can see you boys are having fun," Willow said coming to stand to the side of Millie's bound body and grabbing a handful of Millie's thick booty, slapping it a few times as she looked at her being taken from both ends.

"Let me know when you're finished. I've got a special surprised for our naughty girl," she said casually as she began whipping Millie's back gently. Millie just swung between the two men, being plow until they were finished. Ben cumming over her ass crack and smiling as he saw his cum drip down to the plug and Harvey spilling from Millie's lips and making a puddle on the floor. Lazily slapping her cheek, Harvey pulled himself from her mouth and watched as Millie gasped for air before walking behind her and slapping her ass with his cock.

"You know what I like about this one?" Harvey said to Ben, who was still standing behind her watching her body shake involuntarily.

"What I like is that she never says no the good little slut," Harvey laughed as he grabbed the swing and pulled Millie back and into his cock.

"Gag her, I don't want to fucking hear her," Harvey said to Willow who just rolled her eyes.

"It's alright, I've got it, open wide pretty girl," Ben said, flopping his limp dick into Millie's mouth.

"Suck it you lazy bitch," Harvey said slapping Millie's ass and getting turned on watching it shake.

"Yeah, that's it," he added, slapping her over and over as he pounded her from behind.

"She likes it, she's not even trying to fight it anymore," Ben laughed, pushing his balls into her mouth.

"Gobble it all up, and maybe your Daddy will give you a treat on the way home," Ben said, jerking his cock and slapping it against Millie's face. Harvey slapped her harder as he came, thrusting aggressively into her as he exploded balls deep in her.

"Enjoy," he said patting Ben on the shoulder as he passed, sitting down on the chair and yawning in satisfaction as he watched Ben face fuck, Millie. Ben finished again, this time holding Millie's nose closed, making her keep her mouth open as she tried to deny him.

"Nice fucking try slut," he just laughed as he filled her mouth before moving back to her cunt.

"Uh huh, my turn," Willow said, starring Ben down.

"She's all yours," he finally said, walking back to Millie's face and slapping her contently. He walked over to the other chair and sat down slowly and took out a box of cigars.

"Were they mean you, little princess? Do you remember what you fucking are now? You're ours, and we will give you all the lovies in the world, but step out of line and we will destroy you, pretty girl," Willow explained as she untied Millie's limp body. Willow helped Millie stand and lay her on the floor, taking a wet wipe and cleaning her before taking her hand and leading her to the king size bed that was set up in the corner of the room.

"Lay down for Mama," Willow said. Millie was in such a heightened headspace she silently obeyed, making Willow smirk.

"Whose little girl are you, baby," Willow said standing over the top of Millie.

"Yours, Mamas and Daddy's. And Uncle Ben's when you say," Millie said in a haze. Willow took her dress off slowly and waited for Millie to have an idea of what was coming next.

"You didn't think I was going to let them have all the fun, did you?" Willow said as she took the nipple clamps off Millie's sensitive body, making her gasp as she felt the blood flow back to them.

"Arms up," Willow gently said, waiting for Millie to obey her. Slowly, Millie raised her arms above her head, breathing shallowly as Willow tied her wrists to the bed frame.

"See, the boys like to play rough, but they don't know something that Mama does. Do you know what is it?" Willow said, kissing down Millie's body and tying her ankles to the other end of the bed. Millie just shook her head no as Willow began to lovingly stroke her stretched body, enjoying how the bones of Millie's ribs and pelvis pushed against her skin.

"I didn't think you would. It's this, that the more gentle you are with your toys, the longer it takes to break them, the more they love you, and the easier it is for you to be in their head controlling them long after you have stopped touching them," Willow said as she began to rub Millie's pussy making her gasp with surprise.

"Yeah, Mama is going to fuck you. It doesn't matter if you find it hot or not, you're mine, and I want you tonight. Are you going to be a good girl for me and stay quiet?" Willow asked Millie as she rubbed her. Millie moved her hips in time with Willow's touch, breathing in ragged gasps as she felt Willow creep slowly into her head in a way

Harvey and Ben didn't seem to be able to. Closing her eyes, Millie whimpered as Willow rubbed her clit gently, her mind beginning to crave the sound of Willow's voice. Licking her lips, Willow bent down to kiss Millie's nipples and tits, Millie opening her eyes as she felt Willow slide two fingers inside of her.

"Shh, we don't want the others to hear, do we? What would they think, they wouldn't understand would they baby? You'll get me in trouble when all I'm doing is making you feel good. It does feel good, doesn't it? I want to make you feel good, beautiful," Willow whispered in Millie's ear as her body pressed against her, the weight of her breasts pressing onto Millie's lungs while her fingers moved inside her, building her orgasm.

"Are you going to be a good girl and cum for me?" Willow said kissing Millie's lips, biting them and making Millie moan and softly whine. Willow kept her soft, gentle pace as Millie started to buck her hips against Willow's hand, grinding down as her orgasm rocked her body.

"There's my good girl, shh shh, it's ok, you're safe with me, you're always safe with me little one. Cute, you've made a mess. I like making your little body shake like that," Willow said, wrapping her arms around Millie and holding her tight as Millie hyperventilated.

"I've never done that with a girl before," Millie softly said, pulling on the ties that secured her wrists, panicking slightly.

"Woman. I'm a woman, baby. Shh don't frown, sweetie, you don't want to get wrinkles on this beautiful little face, let me," Willow said stroking Millie's forehead until she stopped frowning. After untying her wrists, Willow pulled the sheets of the bed back and climbed in with Millie cuddling close.

"Such a pretty, skinny, good girl. God, you are stunning with these big titties and little body," Willow said softly touching Millie as Millie began to cautiously explored Willow's body, making her smile and move, to give Millie better access.

"You don't know what to do, do you baby?"

Willow said, finding it endearing that Millie was so nervous. Millie just shook her head and began blushing, looking down and trying to avoid Willow's gaze.

"Here, let me show you. Do it like this," Willow lovingly said, taking Millie's hand in hers and making her touch her pussy, laughing when Millie pulled her hand away swiftly.

"Don't be so shocked. Of course, I'm wet for you sweetie, look at you, you're what dreams are made of, with your beautiful little face and fuck-able body," Willow said, gently taking Millie's hand and placing it back to her pussy and running a finger up and down her slit. Millie watched nervously as Willow used her hand on her cunt, making Millie rub her clit firmly.

"Yeah baby, that's it, good girl," Willow said in gasps, pulling Millie's body across hers and rubbing her clit again, making Millie gasp but just rock in her arms. Willow pushed her nipple into Millie's mouth as she gently fucked her, enjoying feeling Millie's gasps and moans on her big breasts, sending vibrations through her body.

"Do you want to feel inside baby?" Willow asked as she forced herself to rub Millie slowly instead of the power fuck she wanted to give her.

"Come on sweetie you've been such a good girl for me, don't disappoint me now," Willow said patting Millie's pussy and cupping her gently as she kissed her forehead. Millie just nodded her head and held her breath as she slid a finger inside Willow, making her sigh with relief.

"Good girl, and another one sweetie," Willow instructed. Millie tenderly pushed another finger inside the older woman, feeling her tighten against her fingers.

"Move them like I am baby," Willow said as she began to wiggle her fingers inside of Millie, causing her to whimper as she copied.

"Don't stop baby, don't stop till I take your hand away, ok?" Willow groaned, fucking Millie harder as her orgasm hit her. Surprised that she had cum so quickly, Willow kept fucking Millie until she was a squirming mess on top of her as

Millie's orgasm ravaged her exhausted body.

"Good girl, I'm so proud of you," Willow said, taking Millie's hand away and licking her juices off Millie's fingers. Holding Millie's face with both hands as she rested on top of Willow's large tits, Willow looked into Millie's soul before smiling and kissing her deeply on the mouth. Millie wrapped her arms around Willow, flexing her back muscles as she was held by the older woman, getting so lost in the kiss she hardly heard Harvey clear his throat behind her.

"Ok, time to go," Harvey said, coming over and pulling the sheets off the bed in one fluid action. Millie just lay in bed, her mind racing, her body sore, her heart yearning. *What is that, what is that feeling?* Millie thought to herself as Harvey handed her a bag with spare clothes.

"You'll need to get dressed quickly, the taxi will be here soon," Harvey said. He had already showered and redressed and had been sitting with Ben smoking cigars. Millie looked at Willow and hated herself for what she felt.

"Will, I, Mama um can I sleep in your bed tonight?" Millie stuttered, remembering not to call Willow anything but Mama, feeling lucky that the start of Willow's name was a word all on its own. Getting dressed Millie looked at Willow with an innocence she didn't know she could feel. Willow just smirked and winked at Harvey.

"No sweetie, you need to sleep in your bed. You don't love me, you just love feeling loved," she said, knowing that she had Millie hooked. Disappointed, Millie just nodded and walked out of the room and into the night air.

"Aren't you going to say thank you?" Ben said, standing up and following her outside.

"Whatever," Millie said back, a pain in her heart that she didn't understand.

"Whatever?!" Ben said, making Harvey stand up and storm out after her.

"I thought we'd taught you a big enough lesson but not!" He said, reaching out to grab her upper arm and turn her around before slapping her face angrily.

"Let me go! Stop, red, I'm done, I'm fucking done," Millie said, pulling away from him and running into the night.

"What the hell did you do with her?!" Harvey yelled, running back into the room just as Willow picked up her coat.

"I loved her. While you two idiots were busy hate fucking her until she was so filled with your cum that her pussy dripped for hours, I was gentle; I took my time with her, I made her feel safe. Couldn't you see it, see her need to be held and treasured? Sure she could take cock like a champ, but couldn't you see she fell for you because of the way you made her feel precious? You lost her when you let him fuck her; you lost her when you didn't let her be your baby girl for longer than an hour without wanting your cock serviced. You changed with her just because she never made you wait. You stopped being her Daddy, Harvey and you know it. You just became some guy she let fuck her in exchange for a moment of your softness," Willow said. She pulled her coat tight across her chest as she walked passed Harvey and Ben and towards the waiting Taxi.

Chapter 13

Willow's words cut Harvey to the core because he knew she was right. He had changed. He had become obsessed with only one thing, how many times he could stick his cock inside her. He had walked the two-hour walk home the night Millie had run out on him, and it had been a month since he had seen her. She had come to pick up her things, moving back into her apartment the day after that night. Willow had moved out too, but to where, Harvey didn't know or particularly care. He had let them both down; he had let himself down. *Too much of a good thing hey*, he thought to himself as he repositioned a new client who had shamelessly flirted with him the whole training session.

Millie had come home early from work on a sunny

afternoon to find Willow resting on her car bonnet, the fall sun making her raven hair even more beautiful.

"Hey," Millie happily gasped, seeing Willow outside her door.

"Hi," Willow replied, getting up and walking over to Millie.

"I'm not coming back this time. Willow, I can't," Millie said making it a point to say Willow's name.

"I know. I'm not here for that. I'm here to make sure you're ok," Willow replied as Millie stopped outside her door.

"Did Harvey send you?" Millie said, turning to face Willow. Their time together flashed through Millie's thoughts, and she had to shake her head, trying to shake them from her mind.

"No. Has he come to check on you?" Willow asked, putting her hands in her pockets. Millie just shook her head no.

"Cold. He should have. Look, I'm sorry it all ended like it did. I hope you know not all Daddies are like that. He used to be awesome, I don't know what happened, but I'm sorry he turned into something cold with you. You didn't deserve that," Willow said, making Millie smile.

"I never thought I'd hear you say all that," she said shocked that Willow was so honest with her.

"Well it's true so," Willow said watching as the clouds moved over the sun. Millie looked at her and smiled, thinking of how she had changed in the time she had known Willow.

"Look, it's fin. Honestly, I'm seeing another guy at the moment, and I'm starting to see the differences," Millie said, looking down at the ground.

"Oh, nice. That's great. So no women?" Willow said cheekily making Millie roll her eyes and laugh.

"No, I'm not gay, I keep telling you that. I just liked you. But that was a different time and different place so," Millie said, trailing off as the sun came back from behind the clouds.

"Thanks for everything Will, it was, one hell of a crazy ride," Millie said, stepping forward and kissing Willow more passionately than Willow was ready for. Taking her hands out of her pockets, Willow held Millie as they kissed.

"Bye Willow," Millie said, unlocking the door to her house. Willow nodded and looked at Millie lovingly as she walked into her house and shut the door behind her. Millie stayed leaning against the door as she breathed deeply, Willow's perfume still in her nose. Sam just looked at her and smiled. He had seen the kiss and pieced together the faces from the stories Millie had told him.

"That was her, wasn't it?" Sam said, coming over to take Millie's bag from her shoulder.

"Yeah, it was," Millie said, content with the closure she just experienced. Sam smiled at her and took her hand, leading her into the kitchen.

"I've made you two types of snacks because I didn't know which one you'd want more. There's honey sandwiches or cheese and crackers," he said, bringing over Millie's sippy cup.

"And of course, juice," he laughed as he placed the cup in Millie's clapping hands.

"Thank you, Daddy," she said as Sam began to take her shoes off.

Daddy's Naughty Baby

An ABDL age play romantic love story about a naughty baby girl who learned that her Daddy Dom could surprise her in more kinky DDLG ways than one

By Tina Moore

Chapter 1

Lola got dressed in the short pink dress that had taken 26 shifts at the hardware store to afford. She zipped up the back, carefully pulled on her black heels, doing the buckle up at the ankle. Taking one final look in the mirror, she smirked.

"Tonight is going to be amazing," she said out loud as she ran her fingers through her straight blonde hair. Grabbing her clutch on the way out of the house, she double checked to make sure she had the invitation, her strawberry chapstick and the clip Jake had bought her for her hair. He had told her he wanted to put it in her hair and to wait for him by the door of their high school building.

"I am pleased to present the Homecoming King and Queen of 2009, Jake Hudson and Lola

Price," the school Principle of Fever Tree High said down the microphone. The student body cheered, Jake took Lola's hand, and they danced as though everything in their world's finally made sense.

That night was over ten years ago, and nothing more than a distant memory as Lola packed up her truck, securing the ropes over her cupboard which was laying in the tray.

"This'll be the last load; after this, let's get a drink!" She called from the tray. Lola had cut the ties of her small town country roots and bolted like an untrained Brumby out of her home town the minute she had turned 21. She only had one direction on her mind, Hollywood. It had been harder for her to break into the scene than she had first thought, and with nothing more than a changed dream and a plan to make it work, she was coming home.

"Good. I still can't believe you want to go home. It's not like you haven't made a name for yourself. Sure you aren't some big movie star, but you've had constant, well-paying work for years now. That's more than most of us can say," her friend Kate said, wiping the sweat from her brow.

"Yeah, I know, but it's time. Living here has been fun, but I want something - I can't believe I'm about to say this - a little more homegrown," Lola replied, climbing into the drivers' seat.

"Ready?" Kate asked, sensing Lola's hesitation. Lola just looked straight ahead and smiled as she looked down the road.

"Ready," she said as she pulled out and began her final trip home.

"Hey man, what's up?" Jake said, shaking hands with the owner of the home he was building. Jake had gone into the construction business, making his way up the ranks from apprentice to project manager. As an established businessman with a strong portfolio of success, he had branched out on his own and started his company three years ago. With his country morals and cowboy manner, it had not been surprising to the town that his company was one of the best performers. He had successfully redesigned the city, modernizing it yet holding onto its heritage foundation, taking it from a drive-by location to a luxury country hot stop, creating a steady flow of tourism.

"Can't complain, won't change anything," the homeowner replied, making Jake laugh.

"Hey, have you heard Lola is coming back home?" The man said, causing Jake to lift his eyebrow in surprise.

"That's not a name I've heard for a while," Jake replied, making the man laugh and slap his back.

"Heard you two used to drive by the river," the man said signing the papers Jake had brought for him.

"Something like that," Jake muttered, remembering how he had held Lola through the night on more than one occasion.

"Well, she's hauled up at her Daddy's. Heard her Mama talking about it downtown. Might be worth passing by, Lord knows you could use a woman. You still talk to Marg Wilson's girl, Tammy?" The man asked, but Jake hardly heard a word as he remembered Lola's sweet green eyes looking up at him like he could save the world.

"What? Argh, no. Thanks for this. I've got to go," Jake said, rolling up the plans and the signed paperwork before shaking the man's hand again and turning swiftly.

"Yeah, you go get her," the man yelled, laughing as Jake climbed into his truck.

Jake drove through tree-lined streets, acknowledging the locals he passed with a casual flick of his hand or tilt of his head. He wasn't sure what he was going to say to Lola; all Jake knew was that he needed to see her. And see her he did! Jumping down from her done-up black truck with the extra wide rims, Jake saw her tanned legs complemented by brown and turquoise cowgirl boots that kicked the dust up when she landed two feet first.

"Damn," Jake muttered his breath, placing both hands in his pockets and leaning forward slightly in his seat as he exhaled. He had parked his truck across the street from Lola's Father's house and watched as her slender arms flexed when she lifted a box that was too heavy for her. Opening the door of his truck, Jake jumped down and crossed the road, the look in his eyes burning with lust.

"Howdy, can I give you ladies a hand?" Jake said, tipping his hat and slowly lifting his head to look Lola in the eye.

"Depends, where do you think we'd want you?" Lola smartly said back, causing Jake to smile involuntarily.

"How about here," Jake said, reaching under Lola's hands and taking the box from her and walking it inside. Lola eyed him, not surprised that he was still in town. When she had left for the city, she had waited for him by the welcoming sigh on the border of their town for three hours before deciding that he wasn't coming. She had turned on the ignition of her old beat up station-wagon and never looked back. That was until today. Today she was looking at a ghost who had undoubtedly become even more handsome than she remembered him being.

"How are you?" Lola said as Jake walked back out to her truck. He had tried to refrain from looking at her face until now; now, he had no choice. Her long waves of blonde hair, and lips that looked like they had a secret that they just needed to tell made him wonder why he had let her go.

"Yeah good. You?" Jake said, his hazel eyes sparkling the way Lola remembered they did.

"You want to get out of here?" Lola asked, taking Jake's hand in hers as though no time had passed between them. As though Jake hadn't broken her heart, and as though Jake's heart still didn't belong to her.

"Yeah, I know a place," Jake said, as Lola's friend, Kate walked back inside seeing the almost intoxicating chemistry between the two.

"Same old Jake," Lola said, seeing that he had taken her to their old spot by the river. Jake just turned the truck off and sat in the driver's seat, feeling more out of control than he had in ten years. Lola looked at him before turning to look out over the river. The day had been sunny, not a cloud in the sky, and the water was glistening with the sun's reflection.

"Remember this," Lola asked softly, for the first time showing him the side of her he had loved too much.

"I remember everything, baby," Jake said as a tear rolled down his cheek.

"I'm sorry I wasn't there for you when you needed me the most," Jake said, wiping the tear away and turning to face Lola. The plan had been to leave together, to start a new life after Lola's sister had died in a freak car crash four days before Lola's 19th birthday. Jake remembered how she had run to his house in the middle of the night and banged on the front door, so loudly the neighbors had called the cops.

"It doesn't matter. I got over it, even found someone new," Lola said, remembering how she had cried in his arms, wrapped in her favorite pink fluffy blankie as her heart broke into pieces that would never heal.

"Someone new?" Jake asked, looking for a wedding ring on her finger. Lola just laughed.

"It's not that far yet, and I don't think it will ever be," she replied, taking Jake's hand in hers and holding it to her heart.

"Not everyone can be my Daddy," Lola said, her wicked grin spreading across her face and eyes catching the first rays of moonlight.

"No?" Jake teased.

"No, Daddy," Lola whispered in Jake's ear, leaning over and pressing her breasts against his arm making him smirk.

"You were always such a playfully little thing, Lola," he said, cupping her chin in his hand and looking into her eyes, watching her as she nodded her head slowly. Leaning forward, Jake pressed his lips to hers, sighing in relief for the first time in years as he tasted her strawberry chapstick once again.

"Daddy," Lola whispered against his lips, causing Jake to open his eyes and see her smiling.

"I've missed you, baby girl," Jake said, leaning back and stroking the side of her face.

"I can see that," Lola giggled, looking at how hard Jake was, his cock pushing firmly against his jeans. Placing her hand on his belt buckle, Lola pulled on it teasingly.

"Let Daddy help you, baby girl," Jake said, unbuckling his belt and unzipping his pants. Lola watched as his cock sprung from his jeans, pulsating with anticipation.

"Do you still like it like this, Daddy?" Lola said, teasing him by slowly licking up his hard shaft. Jake gently grabbed the back of her head and positioned her mouth over the tip and slowly slid into her mouth.

"Yeah, baby girl, time to be a good girl for me," Jake said, in a hoarse voice as he felt her throat open for him. Lola tried to reach for him, but Jake took her arms and pinned them behind her back as he thrust into her mouth, making her head bouncing up and down on his rod.

"You're going to swallow all of Daddy, do you understand, little one?" Jake said as he felt his cock exploded with cum into Lola's mouth. Lola just nodded her head as she was restrained and face fucked, dripping cum from her lips and onto Jake's lap. He didn't care, he hadn't had her for years, and as she gagged on his hard cock, Jake knew he had to have more of her.

"Come here," Jake said, suddenly pulling Lola off him and reaching up her skirt and into her panties.

"Such a smooth little girl, do you want Daddy to play in here little one?" Jake said, pushing a finger into Lola's mouth and making her suck it before gently parting her pussy lips and sliding his wet finger up and down her warm, soft pussy.

"Yes, Daddy," Lola breathlessly said as she felt him enter her. He felt her tighten around his finger and saw how close she was to her limit. Having him back and being back in her little space while she was fucked made her head spin.

"It's ok, baby girl, Daddy, will be gentle. Just say red when you want, little one, Daddy, doesn't want to hurt you," Jake said soothingly before leaning forward and pressing Lola's seat down until she was laying back. Climbing over to her side, he took her panties down and stroked her forehead and hair lovingly as he replaced his finger with the tip of his cock, waiting to see if Lola was still willing.

"Don't just tell Daddy what you think I want to hear," Jake said in a serious tone. Lola just reached for the water bottle that was in the middle console, and Jake felt his cock slide further into Lola as he reached for it and unscrewed the lid.

"Here, baby girl," Jake said, lifting the water to Lola's lips. Drinking, Lola giggled as the water ran down her cheek.

"Thanks, Daddy," Lola said, bucking her hips forward and taking Jake balls deep, surprising him and causing him to moan involuntarily and quickly hump her in excitement.

"Oh god, baby girl," Jake groaned as he felt his balls slap against Lola with each thrust his pushed into her.

"Daddy, you're not allowed to cum," Lola teased, making Jake laugh.

"Oh, little one, it's you that isn't allowed to cum," Jake laughed as both he and Lola came in unison. Panting, Jake pulled out of Lola's tight cunt and squirted another load on top of Lola's heart shaved pussy.

"Damn, baby girl, I didn't think you could be any cuter!" Jake said, wrapping his arms around Lola and feeling her snuggle into his neck.

"I missed you, Daddy," Lola said softly. Jake kissed her forehead and wrapped his arms around her tighter.

"This time, baby girl, Daddy isn't going anywhere," Jake said as they watched the nights sky fill with stars.

Chapter 2

For the next two weeks, Lola looked for a job. She had decided it didn't matter what type of job it was; she just needed one. Successfully gaining employment at a local supermarket, Lola spent her days finding out what the people of her small town used as vices and catching up on the town's gossip.

"Will that be everything?" Lola asked a man who was clearly from out of town. He wore a biker jacket, and the scars on his face made Lola instantly afraid.

"Kane wants to speak with you. Use this," the man said, before handing her a $100 bill for a packet of gum. He had passed her a phone under the note and left without looking back. Taking the tip and phone, Lola quickly placed both in her pocket before her sleazy boss came up behind her.

"Oh, he looks like a nasty piece of work,"

her boss said, squeezing into her station behind her, forcing her to stand facing the next line of customers who had begun to wait for their turn to be served. Turning her head slightly, Lola gave the older man a puzzling look making him laugh.

"Oh, don't mind me, I just want to make sure our newest recruit is alright. You know you can always come to me if you need anything, I can really help you when new positions become available," the older man whispered in Lola's ear, pressing his soft cock into her ass and rubbing himself against her slightly before groping both her ass cheeks with his hands.

"Jack," Lola said, in a soft, slow hiss as she tried to wiggle out of his grasp.

"Yeah, say my name," Jack groaned, before patting her ass predatorily.

"I'll see you later," Jack said, giving Lola's ass a few quick humps before walking away.

"Kane, one of your guys said you wanted to talk to me?" Lola said in her lunch break. She had gone out the back of the supermarket and nervously dialed his number. She knew it by heart. How could she not when they had been together for six years.

"Yeah, I wanted to know if you were settling in properly, heard you had a nice time by the river," Kane said in the smug tone he always used. Lola's eyes grew wide with fear. She had met Kane the first week she had moved to Hollywood. She had been walking down a street late at night when three men had attacked her, taking her handbag and phone before kicking her until she passed out. Kane was the first thing she saw when she opened her eyes again. He had seen what had happened as he ate in a diner and had taken her to his penthouse suite. Lola woke up to ten men standing around her and had begun to cry immediately. Bending down, Kane had shown a side of his heart he was surprised was there as he cared for Lola and never asked for anything in return. He didn't fit the stereotypical biker reputation. He wore the most elegant suits, drove an expensive sports car and only the forearm sleeve dedicated to his gang could give him away that he was, in fact, the kingpin of Hollywood's organized crime. Lola had felt safe with him instantly and had been given her handbag, and phone back along with a significant amount of cash in her wallet she knew could have only come from Kane.

"Kane, I thought we agreed," Lola said, worried he had decided to go back on their deal. Kane just laughed.

"We did agree, I still do, I just want to make sure you remember your part of it," Kane said without a moments pause. He had never been a jealous man; in fact, he had let Lola see many men while she had been under his care. But she wanted more. She wanted to branch off on her own, and that would mean having to have far looser ties to the gang and Kane than she had previously had. He knew it was good for business; he also knew that he had never cared for a woman as much as he cared for Lola.

"Well, I'll be able to start making serious cash, I'm working at the supermarket, the one on Elwood and Fifth, so," Lola said stopping as she saw her boss walk out the back door and eye her greedily.

"Has he tried anything with you?" Kane said, making Lola jump, he could see her from wherever he was.

"I thought we agreed?!" Lola half giggled.

"Please, let me still look after you even though you are all independent and shit," Kane said in a serious voice.

"The cat is in the back, I don't think it's been fed," Lola said before hanging up the phone.

"I didn't know you had a pussy," the older man jeered, standing in the way of the only door out of the small alcove. Lola just shook her head and tried to pass, again being blocked by the man.

"What's puss pusses name then?" He said, grabbing Lola's arm and pulling her into him. She scratched his face which just made him laugh just as Kane jumped the fence and ran at him.

Punching him in the face, the older man let Lola go, and Kane held her tightly, kissing her cheek and glaring at her boss with murder in his eyes.

"Sweetie, you want to take the rest of the day off?" Kane said without looking at her, Lola just nodded and kissed Kane before walking through the door and out of sight. Kane had not dressed in his usual handsome suits and fancy jewelry. He wore combat boots and baggy jeans, a tight black t-shirt which showed his swol, jail made muscles and hadn't bothered to shave in four days.

"Do you like picking on little girls. Does it make you feel like a big man?" Kane asked as he began punching the other man's face. After breaking his jaw, eye socket, and cheekbone, Kane moved onto kicking in his ribs and shattering in his knee cap.

"Don't fucking touch her again," Kane calmly said, casually jumping the fence and out of sight once again.

"What do you mean the cat hasn't been fed?" Kane asked an hour later; he had rung Lola again, this time from a different phone.

"I mean it, from everything I have seen, she's hungry," Lola said.

"That's what I'm asking about, why are you so interested in this cat, she's too big to feed all on your own," Kane replied. Lola just laughed, whenever they spoke about drug runs they always used this code, she had wondered how the police had never caught them before.

"That was not the deal Lola," Kane said, breathing deeply down the phone.

"Are you, are you fucking someone?" Lola asked as she heard Kane's groan and the slap of his balls against something.

"Yeah well, a man's gotta eat," Kane just laughed as he pulled out of the girl he had just emptied his load in.

"Now, the deal was, you go back home and live happily ever after and if you find an open market you tell me, not, you go ahead and try to run it yourself," Kane said taking a beer from the fridge and sitting on the end of the bed of the cheap motel. He hadn't stayed in a place like this for years and had to admit it felt nice getting back to his roots. Kane had come along way from being the son of a whore, a street kid, a punk who used to sell smack under a bridge and run from cops. Now he didn't have to run, he just had to pay them, and whenever they got too greedy, a blue-blooded hero would get the send off a true asset to the city deserves. He didn't have to worry about the politicians either; they were his highest paying clients. Wherever there was somebody they needed to be taken care off, he was their go-to guy. He knew that he was just as expendable as the people he dealt with, but he also knew that after you've fucked enough of their daughters with the videos to prove it, not many senators would try and fuck with you.

"I'm not trying to run it; I'm just saying that I could. Please let me feed this cat, I know you think that only you can do it, but I can too," Lola said, the begging in her voice turning Kane on.

"Fine, give her a little piece of meat and see if she'll purr for you, but back the fuck off if she doesn't, do you understand?" Kane said, waiting for Lola's answer. She thought back to all the lessons she had learned from Kane, how to hustle and hide product, how to smuggle it without anyone even noticing. No-one suspects a woman in the game and she knew that was her greatest advantage.

"Yes, Kane," Lola said before hanging up the phone.

Jake had been around Lola's every day since her return. She hadn't told him about her boss; she hadn't needed too. Kane had taken care of it. She liked being the girl Jake thought she still was, she liked being his baby but always felt nervous when she thought about Kane finding out. Would he think she was weird, she had tried it a few times with him, but he hadn't known what she was wanting, so she had just left it alone. But after laying in Jake's arms again, she knew she couldn't live without it anymore.

"Hi, baby," Jake said, jumping out of his truck and running across the road to where Lola was standing. Lola had decided to wear her hair up tonight in a slicked back pony-tail, and red lipstick, her white body-con dress and red heels making Jake have to clench his fists a couple of times as he fought himself to keep his cock from hardening.

"I thought you'd like it, Daddy, I dressed for you tonight," Lola whispered in his ear as she casually wrapped her arms around his waist and leaned back, pressing her pussy against him.

"Fuck me; you look hot!" Jake gasped holding Lola, getting lost in her big green eyes.

"I could say the same about you, Daddy," Lola said, taking his hand and walking into the cinemas with him. They collected their tickets, paid for popcorn, and made their way to their seats. The cinema was almost empty, with only a few people sitting in the middle as the lights went out and Jake led Lola to a section at the back. She knew that she would be fucked, and her pussy moistening with excitement. Jake took off his jacket and placed it over Lola's lap, moving her, so she was resting up against his muscular torso and cuddling into him.

"Shh, baby girl," Jake whispered as he took out a thick vibrator from his pocket and reached up Lola's dress.

"Naughty girl," Jake teased, feeling that Lola wasn't wearing any panties. She felt Jake flick her with his finger and she spread her thighs for him, trying not to gasp as he began coating the toy with her pussy juices as the movie started. As the commercials played on the big screen, Jake, satisfied that the toy wouldn't hurt Lola, he forced her pussy to take it and shoved it deep inside her. Pulling her close to him to muffle her moans as he turned in on, Jake pinched her nipples through her dress, enjoying how her tits filled his palm.

"Such a good girl for Daddy," Jake said, holding Lola as the film they had long forgotten they were seeing started to play.

"This'll be a long two hours for you, little girl, let Daddy know when you can't take it anymore, and I'll replace it with my cock and finish you off," Jake said, taking out a pacifier and pushing it into Lola's mouth, startling her.

"Don't be naughty for Daddy, or someone might come and see what you're fussy for," Jake said, settling into his seat with Lola horny and moaning by his side.

As the movie played on, Jake let his hand grope at Lola carelessly, only adding to her frustration and as the film neared the end, Lola knew that she couldn't take the teasing any longer.

"Please fuck me, Daddy," Lola said, her desperate begging taking Jake by surprise. He hadn't thought she could be so willing to be taken as she pushed the toy from her cunt and sat her up on his lap.

"You know what to do," Jake whispered in her ear as he pulled his cock from his pants, leaving his full balls under his belt, enjoying the sensation of the pressure. Lola lifted off him slightly as Jake rolled her dress up over her ass before pulling her hips down onto his waiting cock, forcing her to sit on his lap and take him fully, bending her forward, so she was resting her folded arms on the chair in front of her. Pulling her hips down onto his lap more deeply, Jake felt his balls being rubbed by Lola's firm ass cheeks as she ground on him like a stripper. Bouncing her up, he pulled out of her just to force her back down, making her gasp as she was taken from behind. Jake knew the film would end, and knew that he wanted to have his cum filling Lola's cunt before that happened as he sped up his onslaught, taking Lola's throat in one of his hands while holding her down on him with his other as he pounded her aggressively. Cumming deep inside of her, Jake quickly slid a pull-up up Lola's legs and around her waist, rolled her dress back down over her now puffy ass and tied his denim jacket around her waist. Surprised, Lola touched the pull up and wriggled in Jake's arms, unsure of how she felt.

"Be a good girl for Daddy; a little girl always

does what her Daddy tells her," Jake said as the lights of the cinema turned on. He smiled warmly at Lola as he took her hand and enjoyed watching her try to steady herself on her heels as the pull-up spread her thighs.

"Good thing Daddy had a jacket, baby girl, or everyone would see that you are just a little girl pretending to be a grown-up," Jake whispered as he opened his truck door for Lola to climb in. Waiting before she sat down, Jake gently took her wrists and cuffed them to the sides of the passenger seat, surprising Lola again.

"You're not the only one who has a done up truck, baby girl," Jake said, kissing her passionately. Feeling her nipples hardening, Jake knew that he would enjoy what he had planned for her next. Breaking the kiss, he closed the door and walked around to the other side of the truck and begun driving out of town.

"Where are we going, Daddy," Lola asked Jake who just shook his head.

"It's a secret," he replied, pushing a pacifier

past Lola's lips and pressing his fingers against it until she stopped refusing him.

"Good girl," Jake said, patting the top of her head. Lola watched as they drove for another hour, growing sleepy as the tree-lined woods lined each side of the road. Opening her eyes as they drove up a gravel driveway, Jake ran his fingertips through Lola's soft hair as she took in the big red farmhouse they were approaching.

"I bought this property a few years back and have been doing it up slowly," Jake said stopping the car and sitting out the front of the big home with the tall green trees surrounding it as he reached his hand over to Lola's tits and pulled on them until she moaned. Laughing, he got out of the car and walked around to her side, uncuffed her wrists and carried her into the house. Lola snuggled into Jake as he held her and knew that he wouldn't fuck her again tonight. He took her on a tour of the house, showing her the modern, country style kitchen, bathrooms and living room. Walking into an empty room and placing her down on the plush carpet.

"This could be your room if you wanted, little one," Jake said sitting on the floor with Lola who had kicked off her shoes and was trying to take her dress off.

"Here, let Daddy help you," Jake said, pulling her dress off quickly, before taking his t-shirt off and using it to wipe her lipstick off. Watched as Jake's shirt was ruined before her eyes, the same shirt he had bought only days previously. Lola was surprised he would ruin a perfectly good shirt by staining it with lipstick.

"It doesn't matter, baby girl, Daddy has others," Jake said, pulling her into his arms. He had seen Lola like this before, but enjoying how sweet and cute she looked now couldn't compare.

"You are even more beautiful than I remember Lola," Jake whispered into her ear as he cradled her in his arms, making Lola giggle and search for her binky.

"Here it is, little girl. Come on, let's get you bathed and ready for bed," Jake said, standing up and lifting Lola into his arms, before carrying her

to the bathroom.

Chapter 3

"Hey, have you heard what happened to Jack?" One of Lola's colleagues asked, rushing into the lunch room the following week. Lola had not heard, however, had a fair idea of what would have happened. Trying to sound surprised, Lola put her salad down and looked at the woman with a curious gaze. The woman looked happy.

"No, what?" Lola asked, watching as the woman sat down and looked around the room, her voice becoming a whisper.

"He got jumped and has been in the hospital for since Friday. Some out of towner jumped him while he was walking home after his shift," the woman said, trying to hide her smirk.

"He tried it on with you too, huh?" Lola asked, the woman suddenly looking like she had been caught out.

"Yeah, I'm happy karma got him," the woman said before walking passed Lola and out of the lunch room. *Karma didn't get him, Kane did* thought Lola as she smiled and went back to eating her salad.

Lola had the closing shift the next day, and she had been waiting for it all week. Deciding to take on extra responsibilities, she had said that she would audit the storage room. Lola had told everyone at the staff meeting that she would have to stay later and was happy when no one offered to help her. She said goodbye to the woman who had told her about Jack's hospital visit and closed the store. This is what she had been waiting for, the perfect time to case the store to see how she would bring the shipment in and get the money out. Kane had told her to be careful, that she would need three routes if she were to go undetected. Walking into the storage room, Lola saw the shelves of chemicals, brooms, and sponges, rags, and all the junk that was stored in there because everyone was too lazy to put it in the correct place. Knowing that she would have to clean the room and have some data to justify the long time she would be spending in there, Lola took photos of the room and spent them to the man replacing Jack. She also sent the images to Kane, who just sent her a laughing smiley in response.

After three hours, the shelves were cleaned, the chemicals and cleaning products sorted, and the remaining junk had either been thrown in the trash or placed in the correct place. Lola had found a hole behind one of the tiles that could be easily reached and concealed and took a photo of it and sent it to Kane as well, writing a message at how if she were the boss she would seal it up. He replied by saying, *if only you were in charge*, and Lola put her phone back in her pocket after she had baited the hole in the wall. She had placed the change from the $100 note one of Kane's men had given her in the wall and knew that she would now have to monitor the potential drop spot for the next two months. Lola also knew that she would have to watch the shifts for who was working when to see if firstly, anyone knew the hole was there, secondly, if anyone was even looking and thirdly if it was a safe place to hide the stash.

Lola was thinking about Kane when Jake messaged, asking if she was free and if she wanted to go for afternoon coffee. A smile spreading across her face instantly, Lola replied with a time and location.

"You're early," she said, as she entered the artsy café causing Jake to laugh.

"So are you!" He exclaimed, standing up and holding her in a hug. Lola looked down to the object on the table and couldn't help her laugh from escaping.

"You still have this?" She asked, sitting down and opening the photo album they had made on Lola's 20th birthday.

"How could I get rid of it, you looked so cute, especially in all these photos where you refused to smile," Jake said pointing to the photos highlighting the emo phase Lola had fully embraced.

"How did you find me cute?! I look terrifying," Lola said, slowly turning the pages and feeling all the memories flood back to her. The time they had gone bowling and been kicked out for pushing too many balls down the alley. The time they had written off Jake's Father's car when they went drifting and had crashed into a tree. They both knew they were lucky to escape that one.

"Hey, Jake!" Lola said, looking at the photo of her in a diaper that he had stuck to the last page. Jake just laughed.

"Sorry I hadn't realized it was in there, but look how cute, don't you miss those days," Jake teased, causing Lola to roll her eyes.

"No, not really," Lola said, crossing her arms and sitting back in the chair as the waitress took their order. Jake watched as Lola bit her bottom lip and waited for the waitress to leave their table with the order of two black coffees.

"I like this more," Lola finally said, looking down at the album once more.

"How's work?" Jake asked, as their coffee came quickly to their table. Lola just laughed and looked out the window. She wished she could tell Jake of all her plans, how she was getting her first shipment and that her cut was 30% of the profits, and how she had successfully hoodwinked the town. She wondered how proud of his baby girl; he would be if he knew who she had become. She wondered how proud of herself she was.

"Good, hey, can we not talk about it. I kinda just want to sit here," Lola asked, frowning and trying to feel comfortable. Jake sipped his coffee and looked at her over the top of his cup, trying to figure her out before he spoke again.

"I know what you need, come with me," Jake said, standing up and holding out his hand to Lola.

"It's not your dick," Lola said, more annoyed than she wished she was.

"I am aware," Jake replied, helping her put

on her coat and walking her out of the café.

"Are you taking me home, Daddy," Lola said, as she softened the minute she was sitting in his truck, watching as Jake covered her in her old fluffy blankie.

"Yeah, baby girl. I think it's time you let Daddy really take care of you," Jake said, driving them to his farmhouse.

"I've made a few adjustments; I think you'll love it, baby," he said as they pulled into the newly built driveway. Lola snuggled into the blankie as Jake unbuckled her seatbelt, not wanting the blankie to be taken away.

"You don't have to worry, Daddy's got you," Jake said, kissing Lola's cheek and lifting her out of the rig.

"Come on, it's late," Jake said, taking Lola inside and straight to the bathroom. He ran her a warm bath filled with bubbles and watched as she melted into her little headspace.

"There's my little one," Jake said, as Lola began to draw on the side of the bath with the bath crayons he had bought for her.

"Let Daddy, wash your hair baby girl," Jake said, taking a jug and pouring water over Lola's head, careful not to get water in her eyes. Taking the shampoo and conditioner that Lola had told him was her favorite, he gently made her clean.

"Daddy," Lola said, before slipping under the water to wash the final soap from her body and hair.

"I love you," Lola said, coming back to the surface, surprised that the words had escaped her lips. She had planned to say thank you and blushed as the words she had kept so close to her heart for so long were now shared. Jake smiled, his eyes softening and his heart melting. Running his hand over Lola's wet hair, and bending down to kiss her forehead, he winked at her.

"I love you too, baby girl," he replied, taking a dry towel and lifting Lola from the bath, and drying her off. Taking her hand, Jake led her to the previously empty nursery.

"I told you I had made some changes," Jake

said, opening the door and taking the towel from Lola. He had hired an out of town interior designer who specialized in the DDlg kink to design the room. After giving her specifics about the kind of little things Lola liked, he was sure she would love how the room turned out. Stunned, Lola explored the room, feeling overwhelmed and excited all at the same time.

"What do you think, baby girl, if you hate it, we can change it," Jake asked as he watched Lola explore. Lola looked over the mounted walls shelving a collection of stuffies, the crib with the softest, fluffiest blankies she had ever felt and the wall length window where a wide, pink, soft fabric booth was placed. She saw the feature wall with built-in niches that she could easily make forts in and turned around to look at Jake in astonishment.

"You did this all for me, Daddy?" Lola asked, her eyes still gazing around the room in wonder. Jake popped Lola's pink binky into her mouth before answering.

"Yes, little one. Now come on, I need to get

you dressed before you catch a cold," Jake said, taking Lola and laying her down on the booth. She lay down, and Jake watched as she looked out the window and into the woods of his property.

"The windows are tinted so heavily from the outside that you can see out, but even with the lights on at night, no one can see it," he explained.

"Lift up for Daddy," Jake said, watching as Lola lifted her bottom up as he slid a thick puffy diaper under her.

"I don't want that one, Daddy," Lola squirmed, stopping when Jake gently but firmly gripped her thighs.

"Don't be a bad girl for Daddy, or I'll take my belt off and use it to make that little bottom red and sore," he said in a stern voice that made Lola stop fussing and accept the diaper Jake had chosen for her. Satisfied, he let her thighs go, before powdering her and securing the diaper in place.

"Little girl's need diapers for beddies, baby girl," Jake said, taking a navy blue diaper cover and dressing Lola in it. Jake liked that the cover was one size too small, making the diaper push into Lola's pussy, making her squirm as he pulled it up and over her diaper.

"Shh, little one," Jake said, pulling a white t-shirt over Lola's head and breasts, shaking her body slightly after he had dressed her.

"Cute little girl, time for your bottle," Jake said, lifting Lola up and into his arms. He wasn't as broad or muscular as Kane. However, Lola suspected Jake was stronger. His strength seemed to come from a protective place, rather than brute force. Jake lay Lola down on the couch and placed the pillows around her gently before going into the kitchen and making her a protein shake in her bottle.

"Daddy wants you nice and full my little one; I can't have my baby girl hungry can I?" Jake called from the kitchen. Lola just sucked her binky and closed her eyes as she snuggled into the blankies, being taken by surprise when she felt the nipple of the bottle against her lips. Jake skilfully pushed the bottle into her mouth while taking out the pacifier and moved Lola into his arms as he fed her, rocking her slowly and watching as her tummy became full.

Chapter 4

When Lola woke up the next morning, she knew where she was with immediate clarity. As she turned in Jake's arms, sunlight streamed through the window, and she nudged him until he was awake. Feeling between her thighs, Jake smirked.

"Some things haven't changed," he said stretching and looked at Lola expectantly.

"But I don't wanna, Daddy," Lola whined, hoping that she wouldn't have to wet her diaper. Jake just wrapped his arms around her and held her tight.

"I know you don't, baby girl, but that doesn't mean you aren't going to," Jake whispered in her ear as he patted her thickly padded bottom. He moved, so his large thigh was spreading her and began to bounce her up and down, watching as Lola giggled and tried to push away from him.

"You can't escape, Daddy, little one. Daddy makes all the rules, and you will have to wet that diaper before I let you out of it," Jake teased. Lola just whimpered as she knew that she truly wouldn't get away without wetting herself. She just stubbornly shook her head and pouted, causing Jake to laugh and push her off him.

"It doesn't worry me; if I had my way, you'd be diaper 24/7. Daddy can wait, but I don't know how much longer you can," Jake said, seeing Lola have to fight herself not to wet her diaper. Jake got out of bed and took Lola to the nursery.

"What about breakfast, Daddy?" Lola asked as he took one of her wrists and cuffed it to a chain that was secured to a wall.

"I'm going to go make it, but I want you to stay here," Jake said, kissing Lola on the top of her head before walking out. Lola pulled on the long chain she had been connected to before realizing that she could still move freely around the room and reached up for the stuffies that were sitting on the shelves. After collecting all of them, she made her way to one of the niches in the wall and began playing, just as Jake came back.

"Look what Daddy has for you," Jake said, holding a purple plastic plate with a dino pancake on it. Lola excitedly clapped her hands and crawled to Jake who let her sit in his lap as he fed her. Waiting until she was finished, Jake went back to the kitchen to get her bottle. Filling it with water, he smirked knowing that she would be wetting her diaper sooner rather than later

"Drink it up for Daddy," Jake said, holding Lola's mouth open as he forced the bottle into her mouth.

"Daddy's fussy girl," Jake said, rubbing her pussy as she drank. Lola knew it was coming; she pouted as she wet her diaper, blushing as Jake smirked at her, making her stay humiliated, so she remembered who was in charge. He stayed pushing the bottle into her mouth and making her drink until the whole bottle was empty before softening his gaze again.

"Next time, just do what Daddy says, little

girl," Jake said, lifting her up and taking her to the bathroom. He undressed her and took her diaper off, running a shower for her, their old trigger to highlight the end of their play. Jake watched as Lola transformed back into the smart-mouthed, beautiful woman he loved so dearly and smiled as she opened the door and pulled him into the shower with her.

"You've got me all wet. I could have had my phone in my pocket," Jake laughed, as Lola began undressing him.

"Well, that would have sucked," she replied, feeling relaxed for the first time in weeks. Jake watched as she slowly took off his shirt and pants, his cock boldly bobbing out in front of him.

"Where do you want to stick it, Daddy," Lola teased, taking the shower head off the wall and placing it between her thighs, the pressure of the water hitting her clit making her moan instantly. Jake didn't speak; he just watched as Lola got herself off in front of him. Reaching out, he groped her tits, pulling on her nipples and biting them before taking his long cock in his hand and jerking himself. Turning Lola around and slapping his dick between her ass cheeks, Jake pressed the tip between her cheeks and slid it up and down, enjoying her clenching them together as she felt him trying to enter her.

"Are you playing hard to fuck, baby girl, do you want Daddy to show you how bad girls get fucked," Jake whispered in her ear, causing her to push her ass out and begin twerking on his cock.

"That's it, Daddy's little slut," Jake said, slapping her ass until both cheeks were red. Jake grabbed both Lola's hips in his hands and guided his cock into her, pushing the shower head out of the way as he claimed her.

"I'm going to make you my little cock puppet baby girl, by the time I'm done with you, you won't want to move without my huge snake up you," Jake said, fish-hooking Lola's mouth as he began pounding into her. Lola just moaned as she was taken, Jake pushing her onto the floor of the shower and using her ass and shoulders as support as he speared her time and time again. Lola could feel her abs being destroyed but stayed pinned to the ground as Jake finished hard, squirting deep inside of her, making her wonder how one man could have so much cum. Pulling out of her, Jake picked Lola up in his arms and cradled her, taking the shower head and cleaning her as best he could.

"You'll need another diaper little one, I can't have your pussy leaking into your panties," Jake said with a kind smile. He took Lola back to the nursery, diapered her again and this time, dressed her in a fluffy pink onesie with bunny ears attached to the hood.

Lola had gone to work the next day as though she hadn't just been a little girl for the last two days and smirked to herself when people asked how her weekend was.

"Oh, fine thanks," Lola replied to the third person who had asked the mundane question. As she approached the storage room, she saw two familiar faces and left the door unlocked as she entered the small space. Walking to the end of the room before turning around, she saw one of the men lock the door and stand in front of it.

"I was wondering when you two would show up. You can tell Kane that the cat has been fed I'm just waiting for her to eat," Lola said. The two men looked at each other and nodded their heads at her.

"Kane sent us here to make sure, just keep doing what you are doing, does he know you're fucking that guy?" one of the men asked. Lola just rolled her eyes.

"I was never Kane's. So yes, he knows," Lola spat back, angry that her cunt had always been everyone's top priority. Both men just snorted before walking to leave the room.

"It'll be tonight. Come to this address," the man who had done all the talking instructed. Lola looked at the address before putting the piece of paper in her pocket and watching both men leave.

It was 9 O'clock when Lola arrived at the location, and she was immediately surprised.

"I wasn't expecting to see you here," Lola said, walking over to Kane. He opened his arms to her and held her tenderly, his arms snaking their way under the opening of her oversized, stylish jacket and placing the package of drugs down the back of her pants. Kane leaned back and looked at Lola; he could see something was different with her tonight, and it made him unsettled.

"What's going on with you?" He asked, letting Lola go. She stepped back and saw Kane's muscle back-up step forward.

"Nothing, what's going on with you?" Lola scoffed back, insulted that he would question her loyalty.

"If I fuck this, it hurts me a lot more than you. If it's proof you want, here," Lola said, starting to take off her clothes. Kane knew that the look on her face meant that she was hurt her, but he let her prove her innocence.

"Snitches get ditches; everyone knows that.

I can't believe you think I'd do you like that," Lola said, as she took off her bra and threw it in his face.

"Lola, I just had to be sure," Kane said, softer than he had expected he would. Shifting uncomfortably as he saw Lola's toned body, naked in front of him, he signaled for his crew to disappear from sight.

"I just have to be sure, baby," Kane said, offering Lola her clothes back. Lola took them, held them in her hand for a moment before throwing them done on the ground again.

"Do you miss me?" Lola asked, reaching out to grab Kane's hardening bulge in his pants. He was bigger than Jake, and Lola had always had to cum several times before she could fit him inside of her. As Kane reached between her thighs, he fingered her, sighing as he felt her familiar wetness. Sliding his finger in, he was surprised that she was so open and willing to be taken.

"You've had a dick in you haven't you," he said, sliding another finger inside of Lola making her reach for his forearm to steady herself.

"That's the moaning girl I know," Kane said. He wiggled his fingers, happy Lola's pussy started dribbling juices instantly.

"Such a beautiful slut. Get over here," Kane said, grabbing Lola by her hair and pushing her onto the back of his bike.

"New?" Lola asked as he took his fingers out of her wet pussy and shoved them in her mouth.

"Shut up bitch, yeah it's new, and I've been waiting for your pretty little cunt to christen it," Kane said, pushing his pants down and coating his cock in Lola's juices before sliding his rock hard dick into her until she gasped.

"Take all this dick," Kane growled as he pulled out of her and pushed back in, pounding her, making her tits shake in time with his forceful thrusts.

"Cum for, Daddy," Kane said, holding himself inside of her as his orgasm built. He knew he wanted to cream her hard and deep, but as he heard a car approaching, he aggressively pounded her again, cumming quickly and pulling his still hard cock from her sopping cunt.

"Make sure they get delivered," Kane said before pushing her off the bike, pulling his pants back up and driving away. Lola just rolled her eyes, and reached for her clothes, quickly dressing and walking to her truck, but stopped when she saw who was coming in the car.

"Hey, what are you doing all the way out here?" Jake asked, his headlights shining brightly.

"Just felt like looking at the stars," Lola calmly answered, she could feel her panties getting wetter and wetter as Kane's cum dripped from her pussy.

"On my property?" Jake questioned. He had mischief in his voice, but Lola was shocked. She knew Jake's house was close but had no idea the property was so large.

"I actually didn't know it was your property. I guess that's why you came to investigate," Lola replied. It was starting to rain, and a silence fell between the two of them.

"You could always come inside, and out of the rain if you'd like, I've got hot chocolate on the stove, and the fire is burning?" Jake said, smiling at Lola like he knew she would say yes.

"Only if I can have a shower first, I've had a really long day and just want to wash it all off," she replied, impressed with herself that she had found a way to get out of her ruined clothes without Jake ever finding out. She had planned to wet her panties with water from the shower she was about to have and pretend that she had accidentally flung them in the shower and smiled sweetly to him.

"Deal, come on, let's get you dry. I have a cup of hot chocolate back at mine with your name on it in sparkly pink writing. Maybe if you are a good girl you'll get some marshmallows to go with it as well," Jake said, sitting back in his car and waiting for Lola to follow him in her truck. What both of them were wilding unaware of was that Kane had been watching the whole thing from just behind the tree line. *So you're the guy who's fucking my bitch*, Kane thought. He thought for another moment before turning his bike back on. *I'll see you later*, Kane thought, driving off in the other direction.

Chapter 5

Lola stayed the night at Jake's and waking up before him in the early hours of the morning, she quietly got out of bed and tip-toed through the living room and into the kitchen. Making a cup of coffee, Lola pulled her jacket tightly around her wanting to be warmer. She had kept the drugs in her truck, not wanting Jake to find them, not wanting him to find out who she had willingly become.

"Hi," Jake said, startling Lola and making her spill her coffee on the floor.

"Oh shit, sorry," Lola said, putting her cup down and running to find something to clean it up. Jake just laughed as he chased after her and grabbed her arm.

"It doesn't matter," he said, reaching into the cupboard and taking down the paper towels.

Walking over to the mess on the floor, Jake bent down to casually clean it up.

"Do you want to tell me what you were doing out there last night?" Jake said, seeing the look in Lola's eyes and knowing that he was onto something.

"Don't try to lie to me, baby girl, Daddy knows you weren't trying to look at stars," Jake said, handing Lola back her coffee cup. Lola looked down into her half-empty mug and bit her bottom lip. *Fuck*, she thought, submitting to Jake's desire to know the truth, and looking back up at his hopeful eyes.

"I don't want to lose this. If I tell you, it'll be gone," Lola said honestly. Jake just nodded his head.

"Well, nothing has torn us apart yet, so, tell me and let's see what we can do about it," Jake said with an expression Lola couldn't pick.

"I've started bringing drugs into the town for the Venom Motorcycle Club. Last night I was picking up my first shipment. It'll be dispersed tomorrow," Lola said in one long breath. Jake just smirked and went to his office and came back with the package that Lola was sure was still in her truck.

"Hey," Lola said, reaching for the product.

"No, don't. Why are you doing this?" Jake asked, holding the drugs out of reach.

"Because it's easy money, Jake," Lola said, calling him by his name, causing him to raise an eyebrow.

"Well, Lola, I can't let you get any further than you are already in," Jake replied, emphasizing her name in response. Lola just rolled her eyes and sighed before going to sit down on Jake's couch.

"I used to date, super casually, the king of Hollywood, and well, he gave me the go-ahead to branch out and try the market here," Lola began explaining.

"I guess you can't just, give them back, can you?" Jake asked, making Lola laugh.

"No, that's not how this works," Lola replied.

"Look, give me them back. I got myself into this, and to be fair; I don't want out. Do you know how much money I can make, hell, you've got a million dollar baby girl right here," Lola said, catching the package Jake gently threw at her.

"Lola, I think you should go," Jake said, feeling his heartbreak. Lola just nodded, turning to speak but being cut off.

"You don't have to worry. I'm not going to tell anyone. I told you I'd always look after you, and that's what I intend to do. But I have to look after me as well, and that means that until, or if you ever, give it up, we can't have this," Jake said, sadly opening his front door and watching as Lola picked up her things and walked out the door.

Lola delivered the package to the allocated place in the wall and came back three weeks later to see her cut of the profits along with the next load. She had made $50,000 in two months but was disappointed that all her wildest dreams were coming true, and yet the only thing she truly wanted seemed to be out of reach. Kane had noticed it too and had decided to take it upon himself to try and sort out what was bothering Lola.

"You don't need to speak with Jake, Kane. He is clean, Jake isn't like us," Lola said to him over the champaign breakfast they were sharing on his yacht. The simple life had become too triggering, and he had returned to his former luxury.

"If he can't see that you having everything you want isn't a good thing, then maybe I should knock some sense into the boy," Kane said, dismissing the three women who entered from the downstairs bedroom.

"Really?" Lola laughed, watching Kane shrug his shoulders.

"It's cold out here at night," he said, pretending to plead his case. Lola looked out over the ocean and saw birds ducking for fish and kids fishing from the pier.

"What does he give you that I can't," Kane

asked softly, taking Lola by surprise.

"You called me Daddy all the time. I looked after you and stuff like that," he added, clicking his fingers for the table to be cleared.

"I know. But it's not like that. You are lovely, but you're not a Daddy Daddy. You're a Daddy to a hoe, not a baby, there's a difference," Lola tried to explain. Kane just thought deeply before speaking again.

"I love you, Lola. I love you so much that it fucking kills me. And all I want to do is kill this motherfucker who isn't being your Daddy, so this is what we are going to do. You're going to step down," Kane said, pounding his fist down on the table.

"You're fired," he said laughing and emptied his warm champaign over the side of the boat.

"Really?!" Lola questioned happily. Kane just laughed harder before turning around.

"No! You need to get the fuck over this Josh, Jake, Jay, whatever his name is and remember who you're fucking loyal to. You said you wanted in;

this isn't a fucking merry-go-round that you can just jump on and off as it fucking suits. I swear if you weren't so beautiful, I'd slap the stupid of out you. Now get the fuck out of my face and go do your bloody job," Kane growled, scaring Lola who stood up and walked down the stairs, past Kane's bitches and out onto the pier. The kids suddenly grabbed their buckets and ran to the shore and Lola closed her eyes, knowing what was coming next.

"Lola," one of Kane's men said, sadness escaping his voice. Lola slowly turned around, a tear escaping her eye.

"I'm sorry," the man said before punching her square in her face, kicking her stomach and stomping on her legs as instructed by Kane who let him hit her four more times.

"That'll do," Kane called from the boat before walking back inside, his man following and leaving Lola to lay injured on the wooden planks of the pier.

Lola stayed laying on the pier as she drifted in and out of consciousness until it was well into the night. As she opened her eyes, managing to keep them open as she slowly lifted herself onto her elbows, she noticed the yacht had long gone, as were the cars in the parking lot. *Fuck*, Lola thought once again as she began to stagger to where she had left her truck. Sliding into the driver's seat, Lola locked the doors and cried into her hands. It was dark, cold, and lonely as Lola pressed on the ignition and slowly drove herself home. She thought about Jake, how it would have felt like heaven to be able to drive back to him once more. She thought about Kane and how naïve she had been to think she could get out just like that. *What was I thinking?!* Lola angrily thought to herself as she looked at her beat up reflection in the rear vision mirror.

"Not so pretty now," Lola said out loud as she turned into the apartment she had recently begun renting. Slowly taking off her clothes, Lola walked to the medicine box and popped two pain killers and lay down on the couch before flicking through her phone and seeing Jake had sent her a message.

Hey baby, I think we should talk. I think I've got a solution to your problem.

"Would have been useful a couple of hours ago," Lola muttered as she rang his number.

"Hey, did you get my message?" Jake said, picking up the phone on the first dial. *He has clearly been waiting,* Lola thought, a smile escaping her lips as she tried not to sound like she had just been throttled.

"Yeah, that's why I'm calling," Lola replied, closing her eyes as her head started pounding again.

"Ok, it'll probably be better if we do this in person. Can I come over?" Jake asked, excitedly.

"No, now is not really a good time," Lola replied, hoping that Jake wouldn't need to be told twice.

"Oh, ok, well, when are you free?" Jake asked, waiting silently. Lola felt the tears roll down her cheeks hearing the warmth and love in his voice and wished that she had known what was still waiting for her back in this town before she had sold her soul to Kane.

"Baby?" Jake said interrupting Lola's thoughts.

"Yeah, sorry, um I'm off work tomorrow, come around then. At like 10 in the morning?" Lola asked.

"See you then," Jake replied, happy he had a chance to help her.

Chapter 6

"Baby, what the hell happened to you?!" Jake exclaimed upon seeing Lola's face the next morning. She just tried to smile, but the cut on her lip split and started bleeding. It wasn't the first time this had happened, so she reached into her pocket for her tissue.

"Here, let me look after you, little one," Jake said, rushing into the apartment and going into the bathroom. He wet a washcloth, noticing the significant amount of blood that stained the basin before he left the room. Bringing the washcloth back to Lola, he gently held it to her lip and kissed her forehead lovingly.

"It looks a lot worse than it is," Lola tried to say, trying to believe the lie she was speaking. Jake looked at her dramatically before clearing his throat and frowning at her.

"Who did this to you?" He asked, already knowing the answer.

"After I let here, I went to speak with Kane. I told him I wanted out. I'm not getting out," Lola said, looking down.

"Why did you say you wanted out?" Jake questioned, cupping Lola's face gently in his.

"Because I want you," Lola said softly, as she melted into Jake's touch.

"I always knew you could take a punishment, but I had no idea how strong you were, little one. I think maybe, Daddy might need to keep taking care of you," Jake said, feeling the all too familiar protective love he had for Lola flow through his veins.

"But you said," Lola tried to say but was cut off by Jake's thumb on her lips.

"I know what I said. I was wrong. Daddy can be wrong sometimes, little one," Jake said, opening his arms to Lola and holding her close.

"Come on, let me get you into something more comfortable," Jake said, holding out his hand

and standing Lola up.

He walked her to the main bedroom and gently placed her down on the bed. Slowly taking off her baggy jeans, panties, and an oversized sweater, he saw the extent of her bruising. Her ribs were tender and bruised; her thighs looked as though someone had stepped on them repeatedly. Jake felt a rage begin to boil within him, but he knew that right now Lola needed his love, not his anger.

"Shh, it's alright, baby girl, Daddy is here now," Jake said lovingly. He diapered Lola and dressed her in a duck print onesie. He made a nest out of blankets and pillows before turning on a movie.

"Just stay here while Daddy makes some lunch, ok princess?" Jake said before disappearing into the kitchen.

Lola stayed snuggled up in her blanket nest for the rest of the day, happy that Jake didn't want to talk, he just held her, fed her a bottle and stroked her hair as she sucked on her binky.

"Do you want me to go, little one? Or can I

make us some dinner?" Jake asked as their fourth movie ended. Lola snuggled into him and looked up at him before speaking.

"Can you please stay?" She asked Jake, who smiled and nodded his head.

"I think I should it would seem that you get yourself in trouble when I'm not around," Jake laughed, as he went to investigate what dinner options they had.

Coming back with an oven made pizza, Jake cut Lola's into small pieces as another movie played.

"Baby, I know you've only just moved in here, but I think you should move in with me," Jake said, making Lola's eyes go wide. She had thought that tonight he was just being kind, she hadn't thought that he would want her back in his life.

"Really?" Lola asked in her little voice. She turned in his arms to look at him in the eye.

"Even though I look so yuck?" She added, her self-esteem low now that she had a bruised face.

"You are beautiful, baby girl. And Daddy

loves you very much," Jake said, pausing before he said he loved her. He couldn't deny it, even with her injured body, the gang they would have to manage somehow, he knew he still wanted her.

"I love you too, Daddy," Lola replied, shifting in his arms to snuggle closer to him.

"Well isn't this just perfect," a voice boomed over their heads, sending fear into both their hearts.

"Kane!?" Lola said, ripping herself out of her little space. The usual back up Kane had was nowhere in sight, and he had picked the lock on the door to get in. Kane took out his phone and started taking photos of Lola.

"I wasn't sure what it was about this guy that you liked so much, but now I get it," Kane said, sitting down on a chair opposite to where Lola and Jake where.

"Oh, don't worry about the photos, I'll just print them up and put them around town if you try any of your bullshit again," Kane said, looking at Lola up and down.

"You must be Kane," Jake said, standing up to shake his hand. Kane was amused and played along standing up as well and greeting Jake.

"Oh, so she's told you about me," Kane said, looking Lola aggressively in the eye. Before Lola could speak, Jake answered the man who monstered him.

"Yes, she said you two used to date, back when she was living in Hollywood. She didn't tell me you rode bikes though, that's a cool jacket," Jake said, trying to sound innocent of his knowledge of who Kane was.

"Yeah I ride, I rode that bitch a couple of hundred times. Did she tell you that?" Kane said, trying to bait Jake into a fight.

"Oh, yeah, we all have our pasts don't we," Jake replied, refusing to take the bait. Kane just eyed him, wanting to see if there was any challenge in Jake before getting up from the chair.

"Well, you two have fun now, fuck her in her ass, she loves it," Kane said before leaving out the front door, not bothering to close it. Jake, who had been clenching his calves during the entire encounter, relaxed and walked out behind Kane and closed the door. Walking back into the living room, he looked at Lola, and she stared blankly back at him.

"Daddy, I am so sorry," Lola said, tears breaking from her eyes. She looked fearfully at Jake, worried he would be mad at her.

"You don't need to be afraid of me. I won't ever hurt you, even if I get angry, baby girl. Come here, let Daddy hold you," Jake said, reaching for Lola's pacifier and opening his arms to her. She quickly crawled to him, opened her mouth for her binky and let Jake position her where he wanted before turning the movie back on.

"Baby girl, you're moving in with me, and that's final," Jake said, sitting back down and holding onto Lola as though his life depended on it.

"Come on, let's get you settled again, little one," Jake said, lifting her up into his arms and carrying her to the bedroom. Jake lay her down on her bed and began to undress her. Starting with her the clips of her onesie and pulling it from her body. He took her diaper off next and watched as she wriggled on the bed, before placing her hand on her pussy, playing in front of him.

"Naughty girl, you know, Daddy can just," Jake said, pulling his cock out and pressing it against Lola's wetness, making it grow hard as he toyed with her.

"Come on, bend down and touch your toes for Daddy," Jake said, pulling Lola's arm up and standing her up. Obediently, Lola reached for her ankles as Jake pressed his soft sack against her, his cock resting along her ass crack.

"So easy," Jake said, sliding his now rock hard cock inside Lola's cunt, groaning as he took her balls deep. Holding both her hips, he fucked her roughly, pumping in and out as he got off quickly, wanting to use her as a cum dumpster for a moment. Squirting into her, Jake smiled as he leaned back and let his orgasm finish inside of Lola who had stayed quietly holding her ankles while he enjoyed her.

"Now, where was I," Jake said, pulling out of her and going back to dressing her. He wiped her pussy down with a wet wipe before powdering her and fastening the tabs of her night diaper around her waist. He took a pacifier and placed it in her mouth, enjoying the sucking sounds she made while he rolled on her thigh high black fluffy socks on her, next came her white diaper cover and fuzzy pink sweater which he had bought her last week. Although her tits were a generous handful, this sweater made her look particularly busty, and Jake liked how ripe and ready she looked to be taken.

Chapter 7

Jake was on the phone to the best fence building company in town the next week. He had thought that a fence going around the property would look ugly, but after the encounter, he and Lola had with Kane the previous night, he had reconsidered. It was due to take three weeks, and Jake had moved some of his things in with Lola while the construction crew made the 8ft stone wall with built-in electric wiring for added security. He had also arranged for multiple security cameras to be placed throughout the property, with sensors and warning triggers to be activated straight to his phone and the houses mainframe.

"Dogs, we should also get dogs," Jake said over breakfast. Lola just laughed.

"I think the luxurious prison you're creating will be safe enough, Daddy," Lola said, drinking from her sippy cup.

"You are probably right, but let's get dogs anyway," Jake said, flicking through the pounds adoption website.

"Look, these look like they could be alright. They need an active lifestyle and lots of space to run and explore. Plus they are huge. Says they have basic skills but are intelligent and easily trained," Jake said, reading out the description of the dogs. Lola stood up and walked to where Jake was sitting. Pushing him back, wanting to sit on his lap, Lola wrigged as she positioned herself on Jake comfortably before looking at the dogs he had selected.

"They look a bit scary, Daddy," Lola said, unsure of his selection.

"That's the point. I want two dogs who get along with us but scare everyone else. We should go to have a look today," Jake said, kissing Lola's face. It had healed quickly, and Jake had enjoyed testing her recovery with his cock. He had steadily increased the intensity in which he fucked her for the last week, giving it to her balls deep the previous night and deciding she was ready to taken again.

"Daddy wants to see what you've got on under there," Jake whispered in Lola's ear, licking her earlobe as his hands snaked their way to her thighs, forcing them to be spread open. He liked that she hadn't worn any panties, just her oversized bed shirt that he was already tugging off her. Pulling her pussy lips back, he slid a finger from each hand into her cunt and stretched her.

"Such a pretty girl," Jake said, reaching into his jean pocket and pulling out a bunny butt plug.

"Make it wet for Daddy," Jake said, pushing the plug into Lola's mouth and forcing her to suck it. Gagging on it, Lola felt Jake's cock hardening under her and knew that she was going to be used to his satisfaction today.

"Good girl," Jake moaned, as Lola began to grind on top of him, reaching back to spread her ass cheeks for him and twerk on his rod. Jake let Lola perform for him, watching how her ass jiggled with each twerk, feeling how her pussy juices made his pants wet, but mostly just enjoying how it felt to want to bury his cock inside of her but make himself wait.

"Daddy's got a juicy treat for you, little one," Jake said, taking the plug from Lola's lips and entering her ass as her cheeks clapped together. Jake stood up, pushing Lola to her knees and unzipped his jeans. He watched as his pre-cum sprayed onto Lola's face, her mouth open and her tongue as she stuck it out like he had trained her to do. Bending his knees slightly, he slid his hard, heavy meat into her waiting mouth and pushed down her throat until she was gagging around his balls.

"You love a bit of sausage for breakfast don't you," Jake said, watching as Lola's lips pouted around his cock as he slowly pulled out of her, only to ram himself back in, this time holding her head to him as she tried to free herself from the invading rod.

"No, you'll take it, just like the pretty little

slut you are," Jake said, loving while watching Lola's eyes water. Pulling out and watching Lola gasp, Jake walked behind her and bent her forward.

"Show Daddy your pretty princess pussy, baby girl," Jake said, reaching under Lola and placing his hand on the soft part of her abs as he positioned his cock halfway in her pussy.

"Daddy wants to feel how your little tummy pushes out when my fat cock splits you open," Jake whispered while slowly filling Lola as she moaned and dipped her head in submission.

"Yeah, you'll take it how Daddy wants, won't you, baby girl," Jake said, holding her hips and swaying against her while keeping his cock buried up her cunt. Lola knew he didn't want to hear her response by the way he pushed a pacifier in her mouth as he fucked her. Pounding her from behind, Lola made little moans as each time Jake pushed against her ass, she was jerked forward, and pulled back as he pulled out.

"Such a cute girl," Jake said, turning Lola

around and laying her on her back. He lifted her legs, and she held them in place as she presented her exposed, dripping cunt to him. Jake smiled in delight as he saw the cream he just filled her with ooze from her soft pink parts before he placed both hands on the floor either side of her and let his hips drop down forcefully.

"Oh, Daddy is lucky to have such a beautiful little girl like you to play with," Jake said, pumping her harder and faster as he felt his cock explode inside Lola's warm, wet, hole. Pulling out of her and jerking his cock over her, Jake placed one foot on her tummy and pinned her to the floor as he jerked his cock hard until cum spilled down onto her.

"Who is Daddy's little cum whore?" Jake said, bending down to take the pacifier from Lola's lips.

"I am, Daddy," Lola said, as Jake straddled her tits and begun sliding his cum coated cock between her tits. Content with just playing, Jake slapped her tits with his cock, rubbing her nipples with it, making them wet and hard. He got up and lifted her into his arms before carrying her to the bedroom. Placing her down on the bed, he took out ankle and wrist cuffs and secured her in a hogtie, leaving her neck unrestrained.

"One more time, baby girl," Jake said, loving as he stroked her hair. Kissing her forehead before he went behind her once again, Jake placed a pillow under Lola's tummy before slapping her ass with both hands, grabbing handfuls of her soft flesh and shaking it in his hands.

"Yeah, Daddy's dirty girl. Come on, shake that ass for Daddy," Jake said, standing back and watching how Lola skilfully twerked against her restraints, her bunny butt plug bouncing up and down and the cum Jake had pumped her full of dribbling out of her gash.

"Damn girl," Jake said, suddenly gripping her thighs and pulling her onto his pulsing cock.

"Daddy's home," Jake said as he picked her up and turned her over so that she was forced to take him over and over as he bounced her on top of him. Trying to wriggle away, Jake slapped her tits, pinching her nipples and holding her down on him firmer.

"Where do you think you are going?" He growled as he dumped his load in her once again.

"Is it too much? Do you need Daddy to go easy on you?" Jake mocked, pushing her off him and onto the bed, watching as his cock slipped from her used cunt. He uncuffed her wrists and ankles and picked her up, cradling her in his arms as he carried her to the shower.

"Lola, are you alright?" Jake said as he saw the red marks that were still clearly visible on her body.

"Yeah, I love you," Lola replied, smiling and relieving all of Jake's fears. They showered together, Jake playfully sticking his cock back into Lola who just slapped it away giggling before getting dry and dressing in comfy house clothes.

"What should we do now baby girl?" Jake said. Lola just looked at him in confusion.

"I thought we were going to get our

puppies?" She replied, hoping that having dogs was still a plan. Having completely forgotten, Jake just laughed and held out his hand to Lola.

"Let's go now then, little one. We need to get you dressed," Jake said, excited to be getting dogs.

"But Daddy, I already am," Lola replied, but Jake already had her hand in his and was walking to the cupboard.

"Sit down," Jake instructed. He took out a pull up, her black stockings and black cotton dress, black sneakers and a red bandana for her hair.

"You are going to look so cute, baby girl," Jake said, powdering her pussy and pulling the pull-up on. He secured it in place by rolling the stockings up her hairless, soft legs, and pulled her dress on over the top.

"Cute little emo girl, I love it!" Jake said, putting on her shoes before fixing the bandana in place. Lola stood up and walked to the mirror; she had to admit, Jake could pull an outfit together really well.

"What are you going to wear, Daddy?" Lola said, watching as Jake pulled on black jeans, a white t-shirt, and his sneakers, a snapback cap, and a red bomber jacket.

"You forgot this, Daddy," Lola said, passing him his cologne. He smelt like money and responsibility, and Lola loved how he picked her up in one quick motion and carried her like a princess to the truck.

Chapter 8

Two months had passed since Lola and Jake had picked the dogs up from the shelter. Now they were the proud owners of two large Bullmastiffs. One white called Leo and a tan one called Nix. Although to everyone they came into contact with, they showed aggression; they loved Lola and Jake, who had spent all their free time training the two boys to be powerful protective dogs. Lola had also decided to resign from her job at the grocery store and had given an anonymous tip-off to the police as to when a possible drug deal would go down. While she had made just over $100,000 for her part in the deal, she hadn't taken the $30,000 that was collecting in the hole in the wall and knew that the money along with the drugs would be enough to convict Kane and get him off her back.

"What if he does put the pictures of you

around town?" Jake asked when he came home for lunch. Leo and Nix jumped up to follow him into the kitchen were Lola had made soup and pies for lunch, knowing that once they were finished, they would be given the rest.

"Honestly, at this point, I don't even care. I want to be rid of him. Whatever it takes," Lola said, serving Jake lunch. She had moved in with him now that the fence had been finished and the dogs could follow a series of violent commands at Jake or Lola's instruction. It did scare Lola to have such powerful dogs roaming freely around, but whenever she lay on the floor, they would come over to her and lay down on either side of her while she played or colored.

"It would certainly raise some eyebrows," Jake said, patting the dogs while he waited for his soup to cool.

"Daddy, let's just live our life," Lola said, coming to sit on his lap. She lifted up the back of her skirt, showing him her pantyless pussy and giggled as he quickly turned her around and bent her over the table.

"Such a dirty girl," Jake said, pulling his cock out of his work pants and slapping it against her ass cheek, making it stiff. He grabbed the large slice of pie in his hand, took a considerable mouthful before putting it back down and slapping Lola's ass with his hand.

"Bounce for Daddy," he ordered, taking the sweet iced tea she had made and drinking while he watched her twerk against his dick. Groaning at how hard she was making him, he grabbed her hips and pulled her down on his cock, making her squeal as he locked his legs around hers, holding her in place.

"Daddy is going to have his dick up you while I eat," Jake said, bucking his hips slightly, making her feel him inside of her while he enjoyed his lunch.

Finishing his lunch, Jake carried Lola to the couch, his cock still deep inside of her and let her drop down on the sofa.

"Open that hole for Daddy," Jake

commanded, waiting for Lola to spread her pussy lips open for him. Jake just laughed.

"No, the other one," he said, making Lola's eyes go wide. She bit her bottom lip as she pulled her ass cheeks back, exposing herself for Jake's viewing pleasure before he slapped her hole with the tip of his cock.

"I don't have long, don't fight me," Jake said, forcing her ass to accept his cock. Hearing her moans and squeals only made him want her more as he began his slow onslaught, making her take all of him and holding it in her so she could be stretched the way he wanted.

"Oh, that sucks, baby girl, Daddy has to go, but tonight, you'll take Daddy until I am piping my thick sticky cream in every one of your pretty holes," Jake said, as his alarm to go back to work sounded. Slapping her ass loving, he pulled out, his cock still hard, aching for release as he put it back in his pants and walked out the door.

"Baby, Daddy's home, where's that pretty

little," Jake said, stopping as he walked into the living room to see Lola with her arms tied behind her back and a gag in her mouth. Leo and Nix were chained and muzzled, being secured to the floor by a metal stake.

"So nice of you to join us. I was just telling Lola that something very funny happened today. Do you know what it was?" Kane said with a sinister smile.

"No, what?" Jake growled back, looking at Lola trying to see if she was hurt.

"When I went to drop a package off, a package that Lola was meant to be looking after, the police were already there. It was like; I don't know, they knew about the spot or something. But this is the amusing thing, the only people who knew about the spot were me, Lola, and I am now assuming you," Kane said, standing up from his seated position on the couch. He kissed Lola's cheek as he passed her and took out a gun from the back of his pants and casually waved it in Jake's face.

"So my question is this. Who is going to die today?" Kane said, pointing at Nix and firing.

"No!" Jake yelled, seeing his beloved dog fall with a sudden thud. Jake lunged at Kane copping an uppercut that made Jake stumble backward.

"Now now, don't do anything too rash. I was practicing. It was you, or Lola who ratted me out to the cops and only the rat has to die. I thought I was rather reasonable actually," Kane smirked. Jake looked behind Kane to see Lola crying and straining against her restraints to try and free herself.

"I wouldn't do that sweetheart, I have used my last bit of patience with you," Kane said, pistol wiping Lola and making her scream. Leo barked like crazy, making both Jake and Lola afraid he would be next.

"Look, let's settle this like men," Jake said, trying to stop himself from shaking with fear.

"What do you have in mind? See who can make the bitch cum first?" Kane laughed, slapping Lola's tits.

"No. A fight. If you win, you can kill me, if you lose, you leave town and never return," Jake said, trying to sound dominating. Kane just laughed again before sizing Jake up. As he sneered, he put his gun down and quickly punched Jake in the mouth, making his lip bleed and blood fly, splattering onto the wall.

"I thought you said you wanted to fight?" Kane laughed. Jake blocked his next punch and threw several of his own before Kane blocked him and kicked his knee caps making Jake stumble backward. He grabbed the stake for support, knocking it to the ground on his way down and releasing Leo from his trap. Quickly grabbing the muzzle and pulling it off Leo's head, Jake got up and blocked the next three kicks from Kane.

"Leo, kill," Jake yelled, watching as his dog barked aggressively at Kane before grabbing his arm and biting down hard, crushing his forearm. Kane let out a mighty yell, trying to get to his gun with the dog tearing the flesh from his arm.

"Lola, baby, close your eyes," Jake said, as

he reached the gun first, pulled the trigger and waited for the ringing in his ears to stop.

"Leo, drop," Jake said, watching as the bloody mess that Kane had been reduced to lay motionless on the floor.

"Lola, baby girl, I'm going to untie you now, you have to promise not to scream when you open your eyes," Jake gently said as he untied Lola's wrists and took out the gag.

"Jake," she said, breathlessly pushing him out of the way and standing up.

"What have you done?" She quickly added, seeing Kane's dead body sprawled out on the floor. Jake turned to see that Kane was no longer a threat, and saw the Leo had gone to lay next to Nix.

"I know boy, come on," Jake said, looking Leo in the eye and waiting for him to make his way to Jake's side slowly. Jake took Lola's hand, and the three of them walked into the bedroom and closed the door.

"What are we supposed to do now?" Lola asked Jake who had to sit on his hands to stop them shaking.

"I don't know. I have a friend in the force, he owes me a favor," Jake said, not sure if what he was owed amounted to hiding a body. Lola just sighed a sigh of relief but knowing that what was to come next was even more dangerous.

"Someone will step up, and whoever does, will use our deaths as a way to prove their strength. Who is your friend?" Lola asked, hoping that it wasn't who she thought it was.

"Clive," Jake said, knowing that Lola and he had a history. Clive used to live next door to Lola and once Lola had seen him watching her get changed after gym class and from then on had referred to him as, *The Creep.*

"Oh, no, really?!" Lola exclaimed, annoyed that she had just gotten rid of one problem only to have another one emerge.

"He's the best chance that we have. Lola, we have the body of the biggest drug lord in Hollywood dead on our living room floor, I don't think we have too many options, do you?" Jake said, patting Leo's head. Lola just rolled her eyes and shook her head.

"Ok, you're right. Call *The Creep*," she said before standing and going to have a shower.

Chapter 9

"Jakey boy, how are you?" Clive asked, three hours later as he stepped out of his police car. Lola stood there, on the front steps watching Clive with narrowed eyes.

"Lola," Clive said, nodding to her but walking straight past her and into the living room.

"So, as I said, some stuff got real, and well, this happened," Jake said, gesturing to the dead Kane in the semi-dried pool of blood on the wooden floors of the living room.

"Dude, do you know who this is?!" Clive excitedly said, his mouth gaping open.

"No, I just came home with Lola to find him and my dog like this," Jake said, following the story that he and Lola had developed.

"So weird. I'm going to have to take a couple of photos. Yeah, I can see here that there was a break in, which makes sense considering that you weren't home at the time," Clive said, walking around the space and winking at Lola who had come to stand next to Jake.

"Oh, the old prom king and queen finally back together. I tell you what; Jake was a mess when you left, Lola," Clive teased making Jake laugh.

"What can I say, it's love," Jake said, holding onto Lola tight as they watched Clive take some more photos.

"I'll get the boys here to get rid of this and to clean it up for you. It must be so weird coming home to see this," Clive said, looking suspiciously at the two of them.

"Weird. Kinda like when you," Lola said, before Clive cut her off, not wanting to go down memory lane.

"Well, as long as you two are fine, that's the main thing. I'll need to take your statements, but then you'll be free to go," Clive said, as they followed him to the front door.

"Of course, thanks again for coming to soon, I didn't know what to do," Jake said, holding out his hand to shake Clive's.

"Oh, Jakey boy, anything for you," Clive said, smiling the same sinister smile Kane had only hours before.

"Do you think he knows that was all bullshit?" Lola said the moment they were out of the police station and back in the truck.

"I don't think so. Clive is a creep, yes, but he is more impressed that he was the one to find the body. This'll be good for his career, and that's all he cares about," Jake replied, hoping that this marked the end of the ordeal. Lola just looked out the window and watched as the trees fly by, wishing that she didn't feel the need to cry. It had been a hard day. They kind she had never thought would be one of hers.

"Do you need Daddy, little girl," Jake said, sensing she was close to tears. Lola just nodded and reached for his hand, nuzzling into his shoulder and letting her tears fall.

"I'm sorry Daddy, it's all my fault," Lola mumbled, wiping her eyes on Jake's blue flannel shirt. He kissed her head and looked at her in the eye, coming to a stop on the side of the road.

"No, it's not your fault. You did a dumb thing at the start of all this, yes, but you didn't make him do all those things. You didn't make him hurt you, that's on him. He got what he deserved," Jake said, watching as the first of the winter snow fell onto the windscreen.

"Let's go home; we can watch the snow from our bed, and you can cuddle with Daddy all night little girl," Jake said, to a clapping Lola.

"Here's your hot chocy, baby girl," Jake said, bringing the warm liquid into the bedroom. He had put it in Lola's favorite sippy cup and watched as her eyes lit up instantly.

"Thank you, Daddy," Lola replied obediently before reaching out her arms to take the cup in her hands.

"I love this. My happy baby girl, the snow, Leo by the fire. Tomorrow I want to take you shopping for some new clothes; you'll be Daddy's little snow bunny this winter, baby girl," Jake said, imagining how she would look. Lola could see he was enjoying his fantasy as he grew harder under the blankets.

"Daddy," Lola giggled, pushing his cock down and making him laugh.

"What can I say, baby girl, Daddy likes what he sees," Jake replied, taking Lola's cup away from her and placing it down on the floor.

"How about you show Daddy why I should buy you everything you want tomorrow," Jake said, reaching out to touch her. He ran his hands over the top of her pink long-sleeved sweater, enjoying how the fluffy material felt as he cupped her tits.

"I like this no bra rule I gave you, it's good," Jake said, groping at her predatorily. Lola just giggled as she tried to pull away.

"No, you'll give Daddy everything little

one," Jake said, taking both her wrists in one of his hands as the other hand reached under her sweater to touch her naked skin.

"So soft and warm," he muttered, getting lost as his hand was filled with Lola's left then right breast. Lifting the sweater off her, he sat back and placed her on top of him, watching as she began moving in a slow rhythm on his lap.

"I could just slide into you right now," Jake said, getting lost in Lola's eyes as he slowly pulled his cock and swollen balls from his black sweat pants. Lifting the front of Lola's short skirt up, he watched as his cock gently smacked the front of her shaven pussy, pink puffy pussy lips parting around his thick shaft.

"Don't stop," Jake said, loving how Lola bent forward to rest her hands on his chest. She lifted up slightly, enough for Jake to position his cock under her and lifted his hips up, taking his prize. Lola's pussy, as wet as ever, never denying him as she took him in one slow go, letting him fill her to her hilt and tightening her cunt around him.

"Hold on, baby girl," Jake said as he picked Lola up and carried her to the wall, pressing against her as he began to fuck her in the air. Holding her up by her ass, Lola wrapped her arms around Jake's neck and held on as he had his way with her. Her body becoming limp in his arms as he used her, pounding hard while his balls were wet with the cum that dripped from her cunt, and into her ass.

"God you are perfect," Jake said, cumming again. He lay her on her tummy, pulling up a pair of lace panties taking her by surprise.

"Don't you dare fucking move," Jake said, straddling her thighs as he came to sit behind her. He ran his hands over her now panty covered ass, feeling the smooth, cool material and watching as his cock dripped cum onto them. He lifted the left side of the panties, fingering Lola's closed cunt and wriggling his finger inside of her, enjoying how tight she was. Taking his finger out, he pulled on the panties until they were up her ass crack before sliding his cock along the crevice he had made, pushing his big mushroom tip along her wet crack, the panties holding his rod in place.

"I just want to fuck you," Jake moaned as he began humping her from behind, pushing his cock into whichever hole would have him first. Her cunt opened around his shaft, and he plowed inside, keeping Lola's thighs squeezed together and panties on. Getting onto his knees, Jake fucked her deeper, pushing her head down and pulling out just as he came, deciding to cum on her panties instead.

"Yeah, such a dirty slut for Daddy aren't you," Jake said before going back for more. This time, he shoved his dick into her ass, making her scream as he forced her open.

"Take it, bitch, you love it, you love being used like a dirty whore; don't you," Jake said, taking Lola's hands and filling them with his balls.

"Play with my sack," he instructed as he pushed into her, pushing his balls into her hands and holding himself inside of her as he came. Pulling out, he turned her over and looked at her before standing on top of her and lowering his balls into her mouth.

"Open wide for Daddy," Jake said, placing his hand on Lola's throat and choking her gently as she sucked his balls until he came again, this time letting his cum cover her tits and tummy.

"Good girl," Jake said, standing back up and walking over to the bed and fishing for something in the sheets. He took out a chastity belt which had a vibrating dildo and butt plug, before also taking out a diaper from the cupboard.

"Come to Daddy, princess, I have a special treat for you," Jake said, grabbing Lola's ankle and pulling her to him. He didn't bother lubing it as it slid into her holes easily, making him laugh. Next, he locked it in place, telling her that it would stay on all night. Taking the diaper, he added extra padding, forcing her thighs to spread wide and dressed her in her white bunny onesie. Lola could feel her cunt ache for release as Jake only turned it on a low setting, making her grind on his thigh, desperate to cum.

"No, no cummies for you tonight little girl, Daddy is too tired," Jake said, pulling the sheets down and tucking her into bed. He held her through the night, stroking her nipples and making her suck him off multiple times, before making her fall asleep with his cock in her mouth.

Chapter 10

"And in breaking news, the body of drug kingpin, Kane Jones, has been found in a turn of interesting events as the body was found during a drug raid in a small town just outside of Hollywood," the reporter said as Lola and Jake watched the nightly news. Turning the tv off, Jake looked at Lola who just burst out laughing.

"Oh my god," Lola squealed with excitement that they had gotten away with Kane's murder.

"Holy shit. Well, that's that then," Jake said, turning to face Lola.

"What are we meant to do now?" Lola said, for the first time not having anything to either run from or set in place, and she was bored instantly.

"What should we do now?" Lola said again, excitement in her eyes. Jake just double took as his head spun with what on earth Lola could mean.

"Um, relax?" Jake suggested as though Lola had lost her mind.

"No, come on, let's go out, celebrate, get wasted and fuck in your truck," Lola said, grabbing Jake's hands and bouncing on the couch.

"Baby, no, I've got work in the morning. Maybe we should think about you going back to work now that Kane is out of the picture," Jake said, deflating Lola's enthusiasm instantly.

"Yeah, my thoughts exactly," Lola said before getting up and walking to the bathroom.

"We can do something fun on the weekend, baby," Jake said, receiving a fake smile from Lola.

"Yeah, I'd like that," Lola said as she shut the door slowly before locking it. She looked in the mirror and wondered how much longer she could live a life like this with Jake. Sure, he was kind, supportive, loyal, and loving. But he was boring. There was nothing remotely exciting about how he wanted to live, and if it weren't for the way he fucked her, Lola would have left him long ago.

Turning the water on, Lola slid down the wall and sat on the floor, letting the hot water hit her body and warm her skin. She thought about what she wanted to do next. *Why do you always have to be looking for your next hit of adrenaline?* Lola asked herself, annoyed that she couldn't feel happy with a simple life. She was only coming back to this town to try and run on her own, if she hadn't reunited with Jake, she would have been happily rolling in cash and living for the moment like she loved to do. *That's it, I live for the moment, and Jake lives for, a longer moment I guess,* Lola thought as she began soaping her body, feeling lonely and bored all at the same time.

Lola decided to spend the next few days looking for work, convincing herself that if she could find a job somewhere somewhat exciting, it would curb her need to be searching for her next hit continually. Walking from store to store, Lola realized that nothing excited her. As she walked up and down the main street in town, she sighed, sitting on a bench and looking out onto the road.

"You look like you could use this," a voice said coming behind her and sitting next to her. Lola groaned and rolled her eyes.

"And here I was thinking this day couldn't get any worse," Lola said, looking down at the cup Clive was offering her.

"I could always arrest you, spice it up a little when I slot you," he said, taking Lola's hand and making her hold the cup.

"Drink," he said, lifting her compliant hands, bringing the cup to her lips.

"You're such a seedy fuck," Lola said, eyeing Clive as she beginning sipping the coffee but pulling the cup away from her almost immediately.

"There's Irish Crème in this?!" Lola accused looking at Clive as though he had lost his mind. He just laughed and drunk his, before throwing the empty cup in the trash, leaning across with his big stomach pressing onto Lola's tits and looking her in the eye.

"Yeah," he said, smirking when Lola rolled

her eyes and took another sip.

"You looked like you could use it. I've been watching you," Clive said, getting cut off by Lola.

"I bet you have," she said plainly, sipping again.

"I've been watching you walk up and down here, what are you trying to do? Get a job?" Clive asked, ignoring her cheep insult. Looking at him out of the corner of her eye, Lola sighed, dropping her guard and sighing again before turning to look at him.

"Yeah, Jake thought it would be a good idea to go back to work," Lola said, resting her head on her hand, her elbow resting on the back of the bench. Clive just nodded.

"And no luck yet?" he asked, readjusting his holster.

"Nope," Lola replied, reaching back and throwing her empty cup in the trash.

"Well, we need someone to file things back at the station?" Clive suggested making Lola laugh.

"And you have the power just to hire

someone with zero experience?" Lola questioned, raising her eyebrow. Clive smirked.

"It's a really easy job, doesn't really take a lot of training. Plus, we aren't a unit, have you ever seen more than me and the three other guys in uniform?" Clive said, making Lola think. *No, actually, I haven't,* she thought, a smile spreading across her lips.

"When can I start?" She asked, Clive, looking her up and down, eyeing her breasts.

"What are you doing now?" He asked, standing up and cracking his back.

"Um, actually, I'm a little tipsy right now," Lola replied, laughing despite herself.

"Then you'll fit right in," Clive replied, walking towards the old police house at the end of the main street followed by Lola.

"Hey, Jake, I found a job!" Lola yelled as she ran into the house. Running into the bedroom, she saw Jake sitting up and working on his computer.

"Did you hear? I have a new job," Lola

repeated, watching as Jake patted the spot beside him.

"Nice work, baby girl. Where?" Jake asked, putting his laptop down and closing the lid.

"Cop shop, I am going to do the filing and some paperwork," Lola said, proud of herself for finding a job she didn't completely hate.

"Wow, really? Don't you need experience or like, qualifications for something like that?" Jake questioned Lola who just shook her head no, her hair swaying as she excitedly bounced on the bed.

"You wanna fuck now, Daddy?" Lola teased, turning around and showing him her red lace thong as she pulled up her black leather skirt.

"Not right now sweetie, Daddy has to finish this first. Go into the nursery and take out what you want to wear tonight, I think you've been a big girl for long enough today," Jake said, making Lola pout and whine.

"Daddy," Lola said, drawing out the word, coping a slap across her face.

"Don't make Daddy mad; I've told you what

to do, go do it," Jake growled, before gently pushing Lola from the bed and bringing his laptop back onto his lap and continuing to work. Lola rolled her eyes and walked from the room as her phone vibrated in her pocket. Taking it out and looking at the series of photos that Clive had sent her, she bit her bottom lip. *He is just a dickhead. He doesn't know anything*; she told herself as she wondered if Clive had somehow figured out her kink. She looked at the adult baby outfits he had sent her, along with the message, *I think you'd look adorable in all of these.* Putting her phone away, she walked into the nursery and searched for her teddy bear onesie, enjoying how the woman looked wearing the same one in the photo Clive had just sent her.

"Oh, no, I was thinking something more like this," Jake said, suddenly appearing behind her making her jump. He put the onesie away and took out a pink sailor outfit, placing it over the side of her crib and pulling her to the floor and beginning to undress her.

"Daddy, I don't want that one," Lola said, pushing his hands away. Jake just calmly walked to the cupboard and took out the silk ties and whip, striking her thighs as he returned, making Lola roll around trying to escape him.

"That's why I thought I'd need these," Jake said, tieing her wrists to her ankles, exposing her pussy to him.

"This might remind you not to complain to me," Jake said, whipping her pussy gently, but making her squeal all the same.

"Shh shh, baby girl, I'm not going to hurt you, it's just a little reminder," Jake said, smiling as Lola stopped moving and bit her lip as he brought the whip down on her sensitive skin once more. Tossing the whip to the side, he untied her and carried her to the bathroom, running the shower water over her body and soaping her generously.

"Daddy, you're tickling me," Lola giggled, making Jake rub her more vigorously. He rinsed her off, dried her down, and carried her back into the nursery.

"Lay down for Daddy," Jake instructed, pointing to the fluffy pink rug in the middle of the room. Lola crawled to the middle of the circle rug and laid on her back as she watched Jake walk around the room. He collected her diaper, powder and sailor outfit, as well as her white thigh high socks.

"You know what to do, don't you baby girl," Jake said, pressing he pacifier to her lips and making her mouth open. Sucking loudly, Lola lifted her bottom as Jake placed her thick diaper under her and powdered her generously. Tickling her nipples by flicking them until she giggled, Jake then fastened the tabs of the diaper and rolled her socks up her thighs, pulling them slightly higher than they needed to go. He lifted her onto his lap and held her on top of his knees as he clipped the outfit up Lola's back and ruffled the skirt over her diaper.

"Daddy," Lola said, blushing as Jake toyed with her. He smiled as he placed her back down on the floor and walked over to the rocking chair, sitting down and watching as she started to color in her coloring in books.

"Daddy has to go out of town for a couple of nights baby," he said, rocking back and forth and waiting for Lola to turn around and look at him.

"Why, Daddy?" Lola asked, taking her pacifier out and putting it down on her coloring in table.

"There's an excellent conference happening next week that I think would be beneficial for the business," Jake said, patting his lap and watching as Lola crawled to him. Bending down, he picked her up and placed her on his lap, rocking her in his arms.

"Ok, Daddy," Lola said, burying her face in his neck.

"It's ok baby; you'll be fine. You have your new job, and Leo, you won't even know I'm gone," Jake said to which Lola doubted very much.

Chapter 11

Jake was going to be away for five days. He had told her he would message, but as the second day of his trip started, she hadn't received one text despite messaging him several times. Bored, Lola knew why she had agreed to meet up with Clive after dark and outside of work, but she wasn't sure why it excited her so much. He wasn't like Jake or even Kane. Sure he was handsome but in an ugly sexy kind of way. His thick black beard made him look intimidating, and his hairy, big body made him look like a cave-man. She hated herself for wondering how big his dick was, but she was sure he wouldn't shave there if he didn't shave anywhere else.

Maybe he has figured out that it was Jake who had killed Kane, Lola nervously thought as she approached the quiet bar. Opening the door her heels were the only sound to be heard as she made her way to the back booth Clive was already sitting in.

"Hi," Lola said to Clive, who just pushed a phone across the table to her. Lola recognized it immediately.

"You won't believe the kind of filth that was on his phone. You do know who I'm talking about, don't you?" Clive said, finishing his second beer and ordering another.

"It's not what it looks like," Lola said making Clive augh.

"Oh, it's exactly what it looks like. Why do you think I sent you those outfit suggestions?" He replied, sitting back and admiring the dress Lola had worn. It was red, short but not sluty and he wondered how easy it would be to get her naked.

"Look. Jake is a good guy; he would be ruined if these photos were to emerge," Clive said, looking at Lola predatorily.

"What do you want?" Lola said, knowing what Clive was going to say before he opened his mouth. In all the years she had lived next to Clive, the only thing he had ever wanted was to get close to her. Now, sitting here in the empty, dark bar with the perfect blackmail, Lola knew she was about to give him what he had always wanted. Clive stroked his thick black beard and placed his hand out of sight. Lola knew it would be on his cock, stroking it over his trousers by the way his bicep was moving.

"I want you to get on your knees right now and suck my dick," Clive said without skipping a beat. Lola looked around. Clive must have paid off the barkeeper because not even he was insight anymore. Sighing, Lola moved over to where Clive was sitting, stopping when he reached out to grab her hand.

"No, I want you to sit here, and let me touch your tits," he said, changing his mind. Clive reached out his hand and groaned as he cupped Lola's pushed out tits. She knew she had to give him a good time, or those photos would be everywhere. Staying still and quiet, Clive groped at her while he drank, watching the football on the tv as his cock grew hard.

"I don't even know where I want to start with you," he whispered in her ear, reaching under her dress and feeling her thighs and cunt.

"Spread your thighs for, Daddy," Clive said, smirking as he said, Daddy.

"That's what you like isn't it, a big strong Daddy to look after you, little Lola," Clive said, feeling how Lola's breathing quicken. She hated herself for enjoying this, but as his big hands pawed at her, she could feel her cunt begin to moisten.

"Well, tonight you'll have a real Daddy. Yeah, I want to get you all sloppy with my cum, have your fingers running through my fur as I breed you," Clive said, unzipping his trousers and grabbing the back of Lola's head, making her stare at his long pubes covering his balls which pushed out around the un-cut cock he jerked in his hand.

"You are going to want me again and again. You are going to wish you had given yourself to me sooner after I'm done with you," Clive said, pushing Lola's head down and rubbing his foreskin over her lips.

"The longer you fight me, the longer I'm going to keep you," Clive said, holding Lola's nose closed and making her open her mouth for air. He took the opportunity to stick his fat cock into her mouth, pulling out his balls and rubbing them as she was forced to suck him. Clive only had to pull Lola's head up and down a few times before she opened her throat and took him until his balls were touching her lips, his pubes tickling her face.

"Holy shit, baby, yeah, suck your Daddy," Clive said, surprised Lola was taking him without his force.

"Oh yeah, you like Daddy, don't you. You want to suck the cum out of this dick," Clive said, reaching down to grope Lola's tits once again. Suddenly pulling her head back, Clive pulled his cock from her mouth as he came. Holding her jaw open, he shot his thick creamy load down her, making her eyes water as it tickled the back of her throat. Clive held her in position until he was finished, his cock limp but his adrenaline pumping.

"Come with me," Clive said, taking Lola's hand and leading her out of the bar. As he grabbed his coat by the door, he put his cock away and zipped up his trousers before pushing the door open and leading Lola to his car.

"I know you liked that, I could feel it, you want me," Clive said as he drove through the night. He lifted Lola's dress and caressed her soft thigh while he spoke.

"Look at you; you can't even deny it," Clive happily said as he saw Lola spread her thighs for him. Reaching for her sweet spot, Clive pulled her thong aside and dipped his two fingers into her wet gash.

"I told you, I knew you were wet for me," Clive said, laughing as Lola rolled her eyes at him.

"They only reason I am letting you have your fun is that I want those photos deleted," Lola tried to say although her words came out in moans as she let Clive fiddle with her clit and pussy lips.

Driving over a bump, Clive used the opportunity to slide his finger into her cunt and force her to sit on his hand while his fingers wriggled inside of her for the rest of the drive.

"Where are we going?" Lola said breathlessly as her orgasm built inside of her.

"Just a little further," Clive said as he drove into the woods. Lola didn't see where she was as she closed her eyes and came in Clive's hand, making him laugh in satisfaction.

"Follow me," Clive said as he took his hand away, turned the car off, and opened the door. Lola followed, running around to grab his hand, surprising both Clive and herself.

"What, I'm scared," Lola said in a bratty tone she hadn't realized she had. Clive just grunted as the feeling of dominance flowed through him as he led her deeper into the woods, wrapping his hairy arm around her and pulling her into his chubby stomach as they walked.

Stopping at a clearing, a modest wood cabin with smoke coming from the chimney made Lola stop in her tracks.

"I know this place," she said, trying to remember when she had been here.

"I know you do. It's where we use to play," Clive said, happy she remembered.

"You've done it up?" Lola asked, following Clive inside. She looked around the living space; the rustic feel of the cabin made her feel right at home. The animal hides on the roughly leveled wooden floor, the big soft sofa in front of the fire and the upstairs loft made Lola annoyed she liked it so much.

"You're not going to need this anymore," Clive said, coming behind her and taking her coat from her shoulders. He wrapped his arm around her waist and flung her over his shoulder as he carried her caveman style to the rugs in front of the fire.

"Take your shoes off," he instructed, sitting on the sofa and watching as she obeyed him. Lola rested both her hands on his knees as she kicked off her heels, showing him down her dress. Clive leaned back, his large body melting into the material of the sofa, making him look soft and even chubbier.

"Now your dress," he said, reaching up to turn Lola around, so she was facing away from him. He watched as her dress slipped off her hips, the fire illuminating her slender form. Clive smiled as he saw she wasn't wearing a bra and snorted with excitement.

"You are just a fat, hairy pig," Lola said, as Clive grabbed her arm and made her sit on his lap.

"And how does it feel to know you want me more than your pretty boy?" Clive replied, pulling her back onto him and holding her there, her arms pinned by her sides, her ass being poked with his big, soft cock. Lola just squirmed on his lap, making him laugh.

"Do you like pretending you don't want it? Does that turn you on?" Clive said, making Lola annoyed that he could read her so well.

"Is that why you stayed with Kane for all those years? So you were able to be taken by him whenever he wanted his dick wet? Do you really think I don't know that you two had been fucking for years before you came back here? I see you for who you really are Lola. A dirty, horny, desperate little girl who just wants to be taken by the biggest, baddest Daddy she can find," Clive said, letting Lola go as he quickly reached down and stabbed his cock into her making her scream.

"Bounce on it, show me that I'm right," Clive said, as Lola began riding his cock, bending forward to grab his knees and grind down on him with desperate ambition as she fucked his cock. She knew he was right; she had known it the minute she had enjoyed him watching her. Calling him a creep had only ever turned her on. She wondered how he could have seen it when no-one else seemed to. Jake had missed it, Kane had been too dumb to realize, and yet it was the fat, hairy cop who had forced his cock inside her which she now was willingly taking who had picked it from the start.

"Daddy's sweet little girl," Clive said, taking

her in his hands and bouncing her on top of him with a strength that surprised Lola. Letting her legs go limp as Clive lifted and dropped her body on his lap, Lola felt her cunt gush, covering Clive's pants as she squirted for the first time.

"Clive, I," Lola gasped, unsure of how he would respond but happily stopping her fears as he exploded inside of her, mixing his cum with hers.

"Oh yeah, that's it," Clive said, as Lola's body dripped with sweat from the heat of the room and the fuck she was taking. Waiting until she had stopped quivering, Clive gently lifted her off him, feeling his trousers get covered in cum as Lola's cunt gushed again with the removal of his monster rod.

"I've never done that before," Lola said, fixing her thong back in place and feeling little for the first time with him. Clive looked at her, impressed with himself.

"Well, you have now," he said, standing up and stretching, his shirt lifting to reveal his furry stomach.

"You want to go? I'll get the phone, you can delete the photos," Clive said, reaching into his pocket and passing Lola the phone. She held it in her hands and watched as Clive went to the fridge and took out a beer. Looking down at the photos of her and Jake, Lola smiled as she deleted the images before passing the phone back to Clive.

"I don't want to go," Lola said, wrapping her arms around the big Daddy in front of her and sighing in contented bliss.

"I told you, you wouldn't want to leave," Clive laughed as he stroked her hair before placing a finger in her mouth.

"But here's the thing, if you stay, my cock is going to fuck you over and over. You're my prize, my trophy, and I am going to use you all night," Clive said, chugging his beer before putting the empty bottle on the bench and grabbing Lola's small wrist in his big hand. He led her back to the sofa, this time pushing her onto the floor and standing over the top of her, pushing her head back until she couldn't move away from him anymore.

"Where do you think you are going?" Clive laughed, taking his balls and rubbing them over Lola's face until her mouth opened and she began sucking them.

"That's it, suck on Daddy's big balls, you'll learn to do that every night now that I've got you," Clive said letting his dick flop over Lola's face as she gagged on his sack. He watched as the fire roared and Lola obediently went from sucking his cock to his sack and back to his cock as he repeatedly pushed himself into her mouth.

"Get on all fours," he instructed, watching as Lola turned on the spot for him. He lay down on the floor and began sucking her nipples before taking her hips in his hands and lifting her up, laughing as her arms gave way and she fell on top of his hairy chest as he lowered her pelvis down onto his. He held her, waiting until she relaxed enough to almost fall asleep before parting her thighs and sliding his thick snake up her cunt, taking her by surprise.

"You didn't think I was done with you, did you?" Clive said as he began to fuck her. Rolling over, he liked how his body pressed into hers, engulfing her as he pumped in and out of her, her hole taking him more easily, her moans only encouraging him. He panted as he fucked her, pushing her down with his stomach as his balls slapped against her asshole with each thrust he used to fill her. Cumming suddenly, he squirted into her, pulling his limp cock out, again satisfied.

"Oh, you are good Lola. I can see why Jake likes you," Clive said, sitting on the floor and lifting Lola up under her armpits and pulling her body onto his lap. Cradling her in his arms, they watched as the fire burned, ambers flicking and crackling before he lay her down on her tummy. He placed one of his legs over her back as the other one made way for Lola's head.

"You know what to do," Clive said, flopping his meat in her face as she opened her mouth and began sucking him off once more as he reached down and slapped her ass lazily making it jiggle over and over.

Chapter 12

"What am I suppose to do now?" Lola said the moment Clive woke up the next morning. He yawned before answering her and smiled as he felt his wood harden. He had dressed her in a short baby doll dress that was one size too small for her breasts, making them pull the material tightly over her chest. He liked to make his women look like sluts, and as he wobbled his cock with one hand and reached for her pussy with the only, he liked that Lola was the biggest slut of them all. She wriggled her pussy down onto his fingers, feeling him securing her cunt to his palm and rubbing her with his opened hand as his fingers moved inside of her.

"You can start by taking care of this," he said, pulling the sheets off of the both of them and pushing her head down onto his shaft. Rolling her eyes, Lola opened her mouth and began sucking the pre-cum from his cock.

"I guess you have two options, you either break up with Jake, or you go back to him, knowing that he will never be able to give you what I can," Clive said, taking his cock from her throat and pushing it down the side of her mouth, enjoying how the skin of her cheek pushed out against him.

"Either way, the choice is yours," Clive said, shooting down the side of her mouth, making her feel like she was being drenched. Clive pulled his cock from her lips, taking his time to rub the tip over her lips, watching how they pouted around his tip, coating her lips in his cream.

"Up you come," he said, finally taking his cock from her face. He pulled his fingers from her, pushing them into her mouth and making her suck her juices off before groping her tits over her dress. Forcing himself into her tight cunt, Clive laughed as she tried to refuse him, only making him spear her harder, flicking her clit with his fingertip, making her pussy wetter than she wanted it to be.

"There you go," he groaned as her muscles gave away, allowing him access into her throbbing cunt. He held her there, on top of him before he slowly rocked back and forth, humping her like she was an animal on heat, and he was the beast who wanted her.

"Daddy," Lola said as she was fucked, making Clive take her arms and pin them behind her back as he mounted her from behind.

"Oh yeah, baby girl, who's your Daddy," Clive said as he smashed her raw, feeling her cunt go dry as she was over fucked. He pulled out of her and cradled her in his arms, his hairy chest and stomach sweaty as he held her close.

"Do you want to see just how cute Daddy can make you?" Clive said, piquing Lola's curiosity. She slowly nodded her head as Clive let her go, getting up to go into his cupboard. Taking out a teddy bear diaper, fluffy brown teddy bear onesie, and a white pacifier, Clive smiled at Lola as he came back to the bed.

"I've got to get you all cleaned up before I make you my precious little one," Clive said, taking Lola's hand and leading her into the bathroom.

"I'm surprised how much space is here," Lola said, taking in the large bathroom. The bathtub was big enough for three people, and the shower was modern, the type without doors. The wall length window overlooked the woods, and Lola smiled as Clive lifted her into the bath.

"I had no idea you were so strong," Lola said, as Clive sat on the edge of the bath with his legs in the water. He smiled as he watched her play with the bubbles.

"What kind of things do you like when you are my little girl?" Clive asked, making Lola swim over to him and rest her head on his thigh. She thought before shrugging her shoulders.

"No one has ever asked me that before, I don't really know. I guess I like coloring in, Daddy cuddles and movies. I like drinking from a sippy cup, and I have a couple of toys," Lola replied.

"Well, we will have to get you a whole lot more, I can't have my little angel only having one or two stuffies," Clive said, seeing his cock go hard.

"Daddy, I know what to do," Lola said, opening her mouth and sucking him deeply down her throat.

"Oh, good girl," Clive said, holding her head to him, moving his pelvis forward until he heard her gag and splashing water on the floor.

"Tell Jake that you have to break up with him. That you've found a real man who can give you what he can't," Clive said, pulling his cock from Lola's mouth and replacing it with his balls.

"Tell him; you need a real Daddy. Not some guy who can't see what you really need," he groaned, his cum splashing in the water. Lola pulled back from him and watched as Clive got into the water with her. He lay down in the tub, making her turn away from him as he positioned her on top. Pushing his cock into her without her complaining for the first time since last night, he trusted his pelvis up, making Lola bounce hard on the meat that filled her. Water splashed out of the tub as Lola was taken, being forced to ride the hairy, chubby bear of a man only making her cunt ache as he overpowered her again.

"I hate that I love this," Lola said, dipping her head and allowing Clive to play with her asshole. Clive just smirked, as he teased her rim, before turning her over to lay on top of him.

"Well, you can pretend you hate it all you want, we both know you really do love it," he said, placing his big paw of a hand on her ass cheek and groping it as she rested her head on his chest.

"Hey, how was your trip?" She asked, making Jake look up from his computer as she walked into the office. Her head was a mess. She looked at the man in front of her, with his kind eyes and gentle smile and hated herself for the knowledge she carried in her heart.

"Yeah, awesome, just what I needed actually. How was your time?" Jake asked, trying to subtly turning off his computer screen.

"It was fine, I'm glad to be back here though," she lied, Clive had to practically kick her out of the house to get her to leave.

"Well, that's good. I missed you," Jake said also lying, standing up and walking out from behind his desk to hug her. Feeling his body against hers, a shiver ran down Lola's spine.

"Are you cold sweetie? Do you want to turn the fire on?" Jake said, making Lola annoyed he couldn't just figure out what she wanted. Smiling, Lola just shook her head, kissing him on the cheek.

"I think I'll just have a shower; I'm tired. I went for a run this morning, and you know that wrecks me for the day," she said, turning and walking out of the room.

He killed a man for you. He was your high school sweetheart. You weren't even coming back for him, Lola said to herself as the warm water ran down her exhausted body. Clive had made sure she had no bruising on her body, but she could still feel him on her. The way his hands choked her throat, his cock squirting inside of her, the way he pawed at her making her feel small and helpless. Her pussy couldn't get enough of him. The thought of Jake entered her mind, and she didn't know how she would tell him that it was over.

"Knock knock," Jake said from the doorway of the bathroom ripping Lola from her thoughts. Turning around, she saw him standing there with her towel.

"You've been in here for an hour, I think you should get out," Jake said, opening the shower door and passing her the towel.

"Really? It's felt like five minutes," Lola laughed.

"Are you sure you are ok? You seem distant," Jake asked, sitting down on the floor of the bathroom while he watched her dry off. Lola just shook her head, making her wet hair flick him with water.

"Maybe you need some Daddy time," Jake said as he got up and took the towel from Lola's hands.

"Or maybe I needed a text or a phone call

while you were away!" Lola suddenly exclaimed, pushing Jake away. He just stood there and nodded.

"Yeah, sorry about that, the time just went so fast that I almost couldn't keep up myself," Jake said, making Lola roll her eyes.

"Whatever, I don't even care," Lola said, feeling Jake grab her upper arm.

"Yeah you do, say it, say you missed Daddy," Jake said, waiting for Lola to obey him.

"But I didn't," Lola said, refusing to give him what he wanted.

"You didn't miss me?" Jake said, pretending to be surprised. He knew Lola missed him, and as he felt between her thighs, he smirked with how wet she was.

"Show Daddy," Jake said, pulling Lola's thighs apart, surprised when she refused him.

"No, I don't want to right now," Lola said, not wanting the memory of Clive's cock to be replaced by Jake's just yet. Jake just let her go and walked out of the room, making Lola wonder if he was mad.

"Then you'll be teased until you are begging to be fucked," Jake said coming back into the room and lubing up her double penetrating chastity belt.

"Daddy," Lola said, pushing his hands away.

"It's pointless to refuse me. If you don't let Daddy stuff you with his cock, you can take this instead," Jake said, pulling the belt up Lola's thighs and spreading her pussy lips and ass cheeks as the toys filled her, making her gasp. Locking it in place, Jake took some heating lube and rubbed in over Lola's clit, enjoying how the belt forced her lips to spread around the material. He picked her up, hearing her moan as he put the setting on a medium vibration and placed her down on the floor, making her face him as he sat on the couch.

"Open wide for Daddy, I told you I would fill your holes," Jake said cuffing Lola's wrists behind her back and pushing his veiny cock into her mouth. Pumping her like she was on loan, he came quickly, not bothering to pull out and feeling Lola's throat convulse around his meat.

"Yeah, Daddy's dirty girl, you like to be fucked. Don't you," Jake said, reaching for Lola's tits and fiddling with her as he pulled his cock from her lips.

"Swallow," Jake said, seeing the mouthful of cum Lola had in her mouth. He put his balls in her mouth, holding her throat, feeling her swallow his cum and gagging on his sack as they were sucked into her throat.

"Oh yeah, give it to Daddy," Jake said, slapping her ass and watching as she wiggled it for him, her own pussy juices beginning to drip from her open cunt.

"I should record this shit, you are such a dirty little slut, yeah, make it clap baby," Jake said as Lola's ass began to jiggle as the orgasm, Jake was forcing on her dripped from her.

"You are such a flirt, teasing me until I pound you," Jake said, sticking his cock back in her mouth making her suck him until he came again. This time, he unlocked her belt, pulled it from her aggressively as he shoved his cumming cock inside of her, and held her down as he emptied his balls deep inside of her.

"Good girl," Jake said, patting Lola's head dismissingly as he got up and walked into the bathroom and shut the door, leaving Lola on the floor by herself.

He has never done that before, Lola though, bringing her knees to her chest and reaching for her phone.

Daddy, Lola text to Clive, wanting not to feel so alone. Happy when he replied straight away.

Hey little girl, I wasn't sure when I'd hear from you again, Clive replied, sending her an emoji of a bunny.

Well isn't it your lucky day then. What are you doing? Lola replied before putting her phone away as she heard Jake open the bathroom door.

"I'm not going to harass you to do it. Let me know when you've told him; I'll be seeing you," Clive said down the phone the next day. Lola had hidden in the laundry room, a place she knew Jake hadn't entered since she had moved in and called Clive, wanting to hear his voice. Lola didn't know what to say; all she knew is that she wanted out. Out of this town and away from everyone. She had the feeling of suffocation all over again. She couldn't figure out if it were this town or her life choices that made her feel so claustrophobic. She imagined her life with Jake, what it would look like, how it would feel then compared it to how Clive made her feel. What spaces he was able to put her in so easily and how he knew what she needed and forced it on her until she accepted. How he had stopped all the times, she had wanted to, but still pushed her limits and made her head spin with ecstasy.

"Cool, I think I just need some space. From like everything, I'm going to stay with a friend of a few days to just clear my head. This isn't what I was expecting, and I just need some time," Lola replied, holding her breath and hoping Clive was prepared to give her what she wanted.

"That makes sense. Just remember, Daddy

will be here for you when you decide," he said before hanging up the phone. *He is a real Daddy*, Lola involuntarily thought as she put her phone back in her pocket.

"Jake?" Lola called through the house, waiting as she heard footsteps coming from the living room.

"Yep," Jake replied, sticking his head out from behind the wall. Lola just smiled at him; he was too lovely, the kind of nice that annoyed her. It had been hot while they were fighting bad guys together, but now she was the bad guy, and he didn't even know it.

"My head isn't in the right place, and I kinda just want to get out of this place, out of this town and away from everyone for a few days," Lola said, making Jake's eyes narrow and become serious. He stepped out from behind the wall and looked at her, waiting for her to explain what was going on.

"What's going on with you?" Jake asked, crossing his arms in front of his muscled chest. Lola just looked around, fixing her eyes out the window.

"I didn't come back for this. I came back to sell drugs Jake, and now I'm in this happy little white picket fence life, and I just don't know if it's what I want. I need something more," Lola said, speaking honestly. Jake just snorted and shook his head.

"You've never been able to settle down, that's why you ran off the first time. I should have known you couldn't do it now either. Go, do whatever you need to do," he said, walking back into the living room shaking his head.

"I just need more," Lola softly said as she looked to her feet.

Chapter 13

What would life even look like, with Clive? Lola thought to herself as she walked through the park. The wind picked up, and she pulled her coat around her more firmly as the leaves swirled around her feet. She imagined living there with him in the cabin in the woods. He'd go to work, and she would stay at home, keeping the fire warm and cooking for him, getting fucked when he wanted and babied the rest of the time. *That's hardly the life I want either*, Lola thought as her cunt got wet with the idea. *Or maybe it is,* she added, noticing her body reacting. *How would I even hide it from Jake?* Lola thought. Jake would find out she was with Clive in about two minutes of their relationship being official and the thought of hurting him even more by living out her happy life in the same town as him made her nervous. *It's not like he hasn't killed a man before, what if that sends him over the edge,* Lola thought. She stopped at a park bench and watched the water of the lake. It was still, and calm, nothing like the turmoil she felt in her mind. *But then, the protection of a cop and the force, he couldn't say shit about what really happened that day,* Lola said to herself, biting her bottom lip and deciding that she was safe from that story ever getting out.

"I don't want to feel this way anymore," Lola said out loud, surprising herself. She heard a laugh come from behind her and turned around to see Clive in his police uniform.

"Then don't," he said, sitting down and taking her hand in his. Lola loved that he just took what he wanted.

"Easy for you to say," she said, glaring at him and pulling away, only making him laugh again.

"You sure do love playing hard to get, don't you. But you're not hard to get, just hard to keep," Clive said, whispering in her ear and licking her lobe. Pushing him away, or at least trying to, Lola wriggled in his grip as he put an arm around her and pulled her into his side, holding her there firmly.

"Now listen here, young lady," Clive started to say, making Lola stop moving, stunned by the words he was saying.

"Is that any way to respect an officer of the law. I might need to search you right here for concealed weapons," Clive said, groping her tit with his other hand, making her whimper softly into his chest.

"That's it, be a good little girl for Daddy," Clive said, feeling Lola's submission as she held still for him.

"How about you come around tonight. I'll send you the address," Clive suggested letting go of Lola and causing her heart to crave his possessive touch once more.

"I don't want to, I told you I need some time," Lola said, her sassy mouth taking over once again.

"Guarded little thing aren't you," Clive said, placing his hand on her upper thigh and squeezing. Lola just held her breath, slightly annoyed he could force her into her little space with just a look and a touch. She hadn't realized her hands were on his lap as her head rested on his chest, her eyes looking up at him and her legs wrapped in his.

"Are you planning to do something with those hands, or are you just being lazy?" Clive said, causing Lola to look at the hard rod that was resting in between her hands. Grabbing him roughly, Lola cheekily looked into his eyes as she licked her lips.

"You don't always get what you want, Daddy," Lola said, getting up to leave just to be pulled back down onto Clive's lap. She could feel him lift the back of her skirt and reposition his cock between her ass cheeks, pushing himself into her pussy through his trousers and making him grunt, happy she wasn't wearing any panties.

"Yes, I fucking do," He said, reaching under Lola's skirt and cupping her pussy, locking her down onto him with his strong arm. Roughly pulling his cock from his pants, he looked around to see that they were alone before leaning back and sticking his cock along her cheeks and jerking into her ass crack.

"Daddy, stop," Lola giggled quietly, worried someone might hear them. Clive just grunted as his dick was pushed against Lola's skin, lifting her up slightly and pulling her skirt to the side, her pussy lips being forced apart as he entered her.

"Daddy, always gets what he wants," Clive said, turning Lola's head around and kissing her passionately as he bounced her on his lap. His thick black beard soft against Lola's face as she was fucked, his hairy balls getting coated in the cum that dribbled from her cunt. Clive pumped her several more times before cumming hard, making Lola's pussy slippery and leak with his load as he pulled her skirt back in place and pulled himself from her. He wrapped his arm around her again as he held her to his chest as she began to cry, for the first time in years.

"Did I hurt you?" Clive asked, concern in his voice. Lola just shook her head and began to suck her thumb, causing Clive to wrap his other arm around her, holding her tightly and pressing her into him.

"I just didn't know I could feel like this," Lola said around her thumb, her little voice escaping.

"Feel like what, baby girl," Clive asked, stroking her hair from her face.

"Safe, Daddy," Lola replied, snuggling into him and closing her eyes as the first stars began to dot the sky.

Chapter 14

"Where have you been, I've been trying to call you for the last hour," Jake said the moment Lola walked into the house. It was late, she knew that, but she hadn't bothered to reply to his missed calls or texts. Sighing, she dropped her handbag by the kitchen bench and ready for what she knew would be a fight.

"I told you, I was out just to clear my head. I know that we have this whole thing going on, but I'm still a 28-year-old woman, and if I want some time alone, that's what I'm going to get," Lola said, sitting down on the couch next to him. Jake had felt this coming for a while. He had felt how removed she had made herself from him; if he was honest, he had done the same. After Kane's murder, things just hadn't been the same. They had both been walking on eggshells, wanting to escape each other, wanting some version of normalcy that never seemed to emerge from their relationship. He had tried to explain it to the girl he had been talking to online, saying that his relationship with Lola didn't feel right anymore but not knowing how to end it with her.

"Whatever, I don't want to fight about it," Jake said, turning the tv on and ignoring Lola who just continued to stare at him.

"Do you want out?" She quietly asked after some time. Jake looked down and wondered what the correct way to phrase his response.

"Lola," Jake said, looking at her like she was acting overly dramatic.

"No, I'm serious. Even since Kane and that day, things have been shit. Let's be honest about that and stop lying to ourselves like it's going to get any better," Lola said, standing up and walking to the kitchen. She took out a slice of chocolate cake and came back to the living room.

"We had fun; we were kids, then I left. You stayed, made this great name for yourself and maybe we were naïve to think that we were the same people we were back then," Lola said, happy that he didn't seem too heartbroken.

"I mean, I was only ever coming back to sell drugs, Jake," Lola said, looking at him with a smirk on her face.

"Yeah, and how did that turn out for you," Jake laughed. He looked up at the ceiling and sighed, feeling relieved she was not making this a big deal.

For the next four days, Jake and Lola slept in different beds. Lola worked with Clive, and Jake stopped making her breakfast. At night, Lola would look at real estate, deciding that she would find a place to stay of her own.

"What about this one?" She said, showing Jake the apartment near where Clive lived. It was small, but clean even though it was an older build and Jake nodded his head thoughtfully.

"I'd like to have a look at it with you. Make sure it has good bones. I could fix up a few things by the looks of it," Jake said, making Lola smirk.

"Once a Daddy, always a Daddy," she teased, passing Jake his phone, the photo of a girl showing.

"Oh, Tammy is calling," Lola laughed, ignoring the warning look Jake gave her and went back to looking at apartments when her phone rang.

"Hello," she said playfully, feeling more settled than she had in a long time.

"My my don't you sound happy," Clive said, down the phone.

"Well, yes, I am actually. I've seen some really decent places. Oh, I told Jake it's over," Lola said, remembering that she hadn't told Clive.

"How did he take it?" Clive asked, hoping that there wouldn't be any drama.

"Good, he is actually talking to Tammy Wilson again. He likes the boring ones after all," Lola said, giggling.

"Great. So, are you free now? There's a party I thought you might want to go to," Clive said making Lola's eyes grew wide.

"What kind of party?" She asked, wondering what kind of dress code would be appropriate.

"I've got a diaper in the car for you," Clive said, making Lola laugh and jump up. She walked into the nursey, happy that Jake had closed his door and was obviously talking dirty down the phone by the loud, deep tones she could hear coming from the room.

"What do you want me to wear, Daddy," Lola said, opening her cupboard.

"Bring you fluffy pink diaper cover, black sockies and white t-shirt, baby girl. Oh, and black binky and pink hair bow," Clive said. Lola collected her things in her bag and put in her blue bunny on her way out of the room.

"I'll text you the address," Clive said before hanging up. Lola grabbed her purse and truck keys before walking out the door, driving halfway out the driveway before she saw the address.

"I know that place," she said out loud with a smirk on her face. She had heard about these parties before. The ones where the town's secrets were laid out bare for all to see, the strictest privacy being enforced and discretion of the uppermost importance. As Lola drove to the location, she wondered who would be there, what kind of scandal she would see, and how Clive had been invited.

"Hey little one," Clive said coming to Lola's side of the truck and lifting her out.

"How do you know about this?" Lola whispered, unsure about why she was whispering. Laughing, Clive took her black bag in his hand and her hand in his other and walked her to the large wooden doors of the old plantation style mansion.

"I'm the one who is in charge of organizing it. I have been for the three years," Clive replied, taking Lola by surprise.

"Oh, so it if sucks, it's due to your shitty planning?" Lola teased, coping a slap on her bottom.

"Someone feels cheeky tonight don't you,

young lady," Clive said, pulling her over to the side of the entrance steps and out of sight.

"Lola, what you see here tonight, you can't talk about to anyone, but I guess me but only when we are in the house, ok baby?" Clive said seriously making Lola giggle.

"Yeah, I figured, Daddy," she replied, standing on her tippy toes as she saw the door open. Clive unexpectedly lifted her with one arm and carried her back into the light and up the stairs. They were greeted by two women wearing leather harnessing, their wrists cuffed behind their backs and gags in their mouths. Their nipples had rings through them with chains that connected to collars around their necks. Their make up was stunning, with dark, sensual smoky eyes staring back at Lola and Clive as they passed.

"They are gorgeous, Daddy," Lola said, turning in his arms and watching the woman standing still by the door as people groped them while they entered the mansion behind Clive and her.

Clive waited until he was in the main room before putting Lola down and pushed Lola gently onto her back, making her the center of attention and blush as people looked at her.

"You're fine little one, no one is going to do anything to you but Daddy," Clive said, showing Lola a soft side to his Daddy self she hadn't seen before. Taking her thumb from her lips and replacing it with her pacifier, Clive undressed her, exposing her naked body to the multiple onlookers. Amongst them, Lola counted the woman who owned the bakery and two of the bar owners, they were meant to be rivals, but they didn't look like they hated each other tonight. She saw multiple professors from the local university and the librarian. *I always knew she was too hot to actually be just a librarian,* Lola thought to herself as she watched the middle-aged woman have her pussy eaten by a much younger man while watching Lola be transformed into a baby in front of her eyes.

"There, my little Lola," Clive said, taking

Lola by surprise. She hadn't noticed that he had completely dressed her as she had been looking around the room.

"You can play anywhere you want, but there are a few other babies you might want to hang out with. Daddy is going to take you to them and then go and talk with a few people, ok?" Clive said, picking Lola up and giving her the bunny she was reaching for.

"There you go," he said, passing the major who was pegging the same boy who had just eaten out the librarian.

Clive passed more girls who looked like the ones by the front door, walking through rooms and occasionally stopping to chat with people Lola hardly recognized. As Clive walked into the playroom, he had specially designed for the babies that he knew who were attending; he stopped, his stomach knotting. Lola looked around to see why he had stopped and gasped as she saw what Clive was looking at.

"Jake," she whispered in Clive's ear just as

Jake looked up to see Clive holding Lola in her baby clothes.

"What the fuck?" Jake said, stopping the game he was playing with the baby on the floor and walking over to where Clive stood. Putting Lola down to stand on her own, Clive blocked the punch Jake threw at his face.

"Now just hang on there mate, we can talk about this," Clive said, trying to stay calm. Jake wasn't interested in talking and tried to strike again, this time Clive grabbing his hand and pinning it behind his back.

"I said, listen," Clive said, holding Jake firmly until he stopped struggling. Letting him go slowly, Clive came to stand in front of Lola who grabbed onto the back of his shirt.

"Well?" Jake said, shrugging his shoulders and shaking his head.

"Well, what?" Clive replied, unsure of what Jake wanted.

"Fucking explain this shit!" Jake said gesturing to Lola, who looked out behind her big

Daddy's back.

"You said he was a fucking creep, remember?!" Jake said loudly, making other people come to stand around them.

"Foreplay is an interesting thing like that," Clive said, enjoying his joke but making Jake even angrier.

"Why do you even care, it's not like you are here alone," Clive said, looking over Jake's shoulder to see that it is Tammy who he had brought to the party. Clive recognized the outfit Jake had dressed her in as one of Lola's, and he bit his lip, not wanting to escalate the situation further but annoyed that he wouldn't have bought Tammy something new.

"That's not the point," Jake said, feeling deflated.

"What's the point then?" Clive asked, seeing that Jake was no longer angry.

"Well, I loved her," Jake said, making Lola's eyes go wide.

"Sounds like it is past tense mate," Clive

said, stepping forward.

"Yeah I guess it is, it's just weird seeing all this, you know?" Jake said, looking at Clive for the first time in the eye. Clive nodded his head and shook hands with Jake as Lola peeped out from behind his back.

"Is that my pink sailor suit?" She asked Jake with narrow eyes in her little voice.

"Um," Jake replied, laughing.

"You never even liked it," he added before going back to sit down next to Tammy and began playing with her again.

"Daddy, I don't want to play here," Lola said, pulling on Clive's shirt.

"Yeah, I think that's a good call, baby," he said, taking her hand and leading her out back into the main room. He set her up in the corner of the room with her bunny and some blocks, coloring in and a movie on her iPad before he made his rounds around the party.

Chapter 15

"Did you have fun, little one?" Clive asked as he buckled Lola into the truck. During the party, he had seen how Lola was sitting in the corner watching everyone get their kink on and had known that she wanted to go home.

"Yeah, but I'm happy we are going now, Daddy," Lola replied as she played with her blankie and sucked her pacifier.

"It is late, isn't it. Daddy will get you home soon and tucked up in bed," Clive said, turning the truck on and driving onto the main road.

"I can't believe that the major was all like," Lola said making Clive laugh.

"And Ms. Williams from the library?!" She added, bringing her knees to her chest and pulling her blankie over her knees.

"Remember, though; it's a secret. The only

way we can have parties like that is because everyone plays by the rules and that means you need to as well," Clive said. Lola just nodded as she put her head back on the seat, feeling how Clive pressed the button to make her seat move backward so she could sleep on the drive home.

Clive and Lola settled into a life of work and play, surprising Lola with how settled she felt with him. She had spent her life running from anyone who got close to her, but with Clive, she didn't want to run. Every time she tried, he would just let her go. He didn't chase her; he didn't try to keep her, he just let her be with him without trying to cage her, and for that, she was genuinely grateful.

"Hey, have you sorted that list of most wanted? I need it on my desk," Clive said, popping his head around the corner of her office doorway.

"Um, no, not yet. Can I give it to you tomorrow?" Lola said, shuffling some papers as Clive walked into the room and shut the door, locking it behind him and pulling the blinds down.

It was late, later than either of them needed to be there, and the change over had the boys in the lounge waiting for something exciting to happen. Clive knew they wouldn't be interrupted as he slowly walked over to Lola, taking his belt off.

"No, I said I need it now," Clive said, repeating himself as he looped the belt around Lola's neck and pulled it firmly, collaring her.

"Get up on this desk," he instructed, lifting his arm, pulling up to her feet. She crawled onto her desk, her knee-length skirt being pushed up by Clive's hand before bringing it back down firmly on her ass, making her gasp loudly.

"Oh, baby, I wouldn't make so much noise. Not unless you want the boys to come in and see you being spanked like the naughty girl you are," Clive said, striking her again. This time he pulled her panties down roughly around her mid-thigh and as he continued to hold his belt in one hand choking Lola, her over spanked her ass red.

"Shake your ass for Daddy," Clive instructed, letting the belt go and walking behind her, spreading her ass cheeks apart and spitting onto her pussy before licking her with his fat tongue making sure she was completely wet from clit to asshole. Lola tried to stay still but pushed herself against his face wanting him deeper inside of her as he teased her with his tongue, tasting her sweet honey.

"Such a beautiful girl," Clive said, pulling her legs back and making her stand on her heels as she was bent over the desk.

"Are you going to stay a sweet girl, or does Daddy have to fuck you into submission?" Clive said, letting his pants drop to the floor and pulling his eager cock from his tight briefs.

"I've wanted to let this big boy worm his way inside of you all day," Clive whispered as he pushed into Lola, covering her mouth with his hand while his other one rubbed her clit as his cock filled her.

"Yeah, there it is, that soft, squishy warm honey pot, give it to Daddy," Clive groaned as he fucked Lola slowly, deliberately pulling out until his tip was being squeezed as Lola's pussy muscles contracted around it.

"Who is Daddy's good little girl," Clive said as he pushed back into her, watching as her head dipped and her breathing coming in short, shallow gasps as he pushed into her hilt.

"Can you feel Daddy. Can you feel it here," Clive said, taking his hand from her clit and feeling for his cock as it pushed out her tummy.

"Yeah you can, can't you. Daddy can feel it, feel how I own you," he said before pumping her harder and faster.

"Remember how the major took that gagged whore? That's how Daddy wants to fuck you today, little one," Clive said, pushing Lola's head down onto the desk and lifting his leg onto the table to get inside of her more forcefully. Lola just lay on the table, getting fucked and cumming more times she could keep count of as Clive pounded her behind. Groaning as he exploded inside of her, Clive pulled out and grabbed Lola by the back of her head.

"Get me down your throat," Clive said, burying his cock in Lola's open mouth, enjoying that he had taught her so well. She sucked him, her lips closing around his heavy rod, making her have to hold his balls in her hand to keep him in her mouth.

"Yeah, Daddy's got a big boy hasn't he, and you're going to make him very happy," Clive said, feeling Lola massage his hairy balls in her small hands. Suddenly pulling out, Clive let his cock swing as he walked to Lola's bag and took out the big pink dildo with the suction on the base, spitting on it and walking back to her. He took her office chair and stuck it to the middle before taking her hand and lifting her to her feet.

"Sit on it," Clive said, standing back and stroking his hard shaft as he watched her lower herself onto the dildo.

"Bounce, make those titties shake," Clive instructed, reaching for her tits and jiggling them, slapping his cock against her until she reached a rhythm he was happy with.

"Now finish Daddy off," Clive said, pressing his tip to Lola's lips and parting them slightly, taking his time, watching how she kissed him. He ran his cock over her mouth, shaking his head when she opened her mouth for him. He didn't want her to be so willing; he wanted to have to fight her today.

"Close your eyes," Clive ordered, slapping her face with his cock as she fucked herself on the dildo. Her legs were getting tired, he could tell by the slowing of her bouncing and picking her up under her arms, he carried her to the couch along a wall and laid her down. He pulled her panties down and placed them in her mouth as he ran his cock over her cheek, making her face wet with his mark.

"Daddy little princess," Clive grunted as he came on her panties, watching his cum drip from the edge of her panties and onto her lips.

"Lick your lips for me," he ordered, pulling the panties from her mouth and drying his cock off with them before sliding them back up Lola's thighs and over her pussy.

"Keep your eyes shut," he said, slapping Lola's tits when she tried to open them.

"Yes, Daddy," Lola said, she felt the wetness from her saliva mixed with cum press into her cunt by the pull-up Clive was making her wear over the top. He stood over the top of her, looking down at a woman he couldn't believe loved him as much as she did.

"I love you, Lola," Clive said, walking over to get his trousers and pull them back on. Lola opened her eyes, unsure of how to process the words in her current headspace.

"Just give me a minute," she said, making Clive laugh.

"It's all good baby, let Daddy take you home and look after you," Clive said, picking Lola up and catching her as her legs gave way.

"Daddy, I think you fucked my abs away," she said giggling as she held her tummy, sore from the hard fuck he had just given her.

Going out the back exit, Clive carried Lola to his

truck and buckled her in.

"I feel like you deserve this," Clive said, passing Lola a box wrapped in pink paper and a big silver bow.

"Can I open it now, Daddy?" Lola asked, shaking the box in her hands, wondering what was inside.

"Yeah you can," Clive said, jumping in the driver's seat and leaning over to kiss Lola's forehead. Lola ripped the at the paper as Clive drove to his cabin in the woods. Although Lola had bought her own apartment, she had decided to make it an investment and rented it out to three college students who paid her handsomely for the privilege. Opening the box, Lola saw that it was the colorful Lama stuffie she had been obsessed with since she had seen it arrive in the toy store they passed on their way to work.

"Daddy!" Lola squealed, hugging his arm and making him swerve as he drove.

"Woah, little one, be careful, Daddy still needs to drive!" Clive said, placing his arm out and over her body, not wanting to be hurt if she had caused him to have an accident.

"Sorry, Daddy," Lola said, instantly playing with her new stuffie and reaching into her bag to look for her bunny.

"It's here baby, remember Daddy took it out of your bag this morning when you tried to take it into work?" Clive said, pulling the blue rabbit from the side pocket of his truck.

Lola played for the whole drive home, talking to each the toys in her little voice and making sure they were friends. Clive played along, enjoying how comfortable she was in her little space. Pulling into the newly paved driveway of their cabin home, Clive swung the truck around and parked it in front of the door and unbuckled Lola before he got out and walked around to her side.

"Come to Daddy," Clive said, catching Lola as she jumped into her arms, both stuffies also coming and knocking into Clive's face.

"Good thing you are so cute," he said, carrying her inside.

"Daddy, Phoebe said she wants dino nuggies," Lola said, as Clive put her on the sofa and pulling her blouse and skirt off.

"I have a feeling that you want nuggies and are making Phoebe say she wants them, so I say yes because you know it's not dinner time yet. Did Daddy make you hungry after the workout I just gave you?" Clive said, causing Lola to roll onto her back as she giggled getting caught out.

"That's what I thought," he said, taking his clothes off and collecting both his and Lola's clothes in a pile and throwing them in the laundry basket.

"Come here, baby girl, you need a bath," Clive said, walking into the bathroom, followed by Lola who was busy trying to take down her pull up and panties.

"When will you learn little one, you are too little to manage this," Clive said, sitting her on his lap and undressing her before helping her into the bath.

"Bubbles, Daddy?" Lola asked, pouting

when Clive shook his head no.

"Oh baby, you little grumpy thing," he said, sitting in the tub behind her and beginning to wash her pussy.

"Daddy, it hurts," Lola said, pulling away from him. Clive reached over to the cupboard, taking out Lola's favorite duck washcloth and used that on her pussy, patting her gently and making her giggle.

"That's better isn't it, little one," Clive loving said, watching as Lola came to sit in his lap as he washed her clean.

"Yes, Daddy," Lola replied, closing her eyes and resting against Clive's bear-like body.

"You can't fall asleep yet," he said, standing up and letting the water drip from his cock onto her lips, watching as Lola's lips parted obediently. Laughing, Clive just took her hands from his thighs and put them back in the water.

"I was honestly just getting out of the tub little one, but you are such a good girl for Daddy. But not right now, right now I want to get you ready for bed and wrap you up in my arms," Clive said, stroking her cheek as his cock rested against her face, poking into her cheek and lips.

"Ok, Daddy," Lola said, going back to play with her bath toys, wriggling her arms and legs as Clive pulled her from the water.

"Daddy, I wasn't finished," she whined, copping a stern look from Clive. He carried her wet body in his arms as he took a new towel from the open shelves Lola had convinced him he needed and wrapped her in the large bath sheet.

"Go and stand by the fire, little one, Daddy will be there in a minute," he said, as he began to trim his beard. Nodding, Lola let her towel drag through the cabin until she reached the fire, warming her hands and dropping the towel the moment she was in front of its warmth.

"Baby!" Clive exclaimed, coming into the room and seeing her naked body silhouetted by the flames. Lola turned her head to see he had her bottle and diaper in his hand and quickly walked to where he was sitting, laying down, wanting her diaper on.

"Oh, you aren't going to fight Daddy tonight? That's a first," Clive said, tickling Lola's tummy and putting her diaper on before cradling her in his arms and feeding her the milky bottle.

"Daddy, what's this taste?" Lola said, noticing that her milk tasted different tonight.

"It's a new protein I'm trying, do you like it," Clive asked, giving Lola time to think before nodding her head and suckling on the nipple of the bottle as she nursed.

"Finished!" Lola said, flinging her arms up and trying to crawl out Clive's embrace as she finished her bottle.

"Hold on, little monster, last time you ran away after your bottle you had a tummy ache, do you remember that?" Clive said, holding her firmly against his torso. He had put on grey sweat pants, his long rod soft under Lola's padded bottom, but his chest bare and hair tickling Lola's check.

"You need to get dressed, Daddy, or you'll catch a cold," Lola said, repeating the words Clive had repeatedly told her.

"Is that so?" He said, wrapping her in a blanket before going to the bedroom and putting on a sport branded t-shirt and hoodie. That was the thing Lola loved about Clive. He had the most expensive wardrobe she had ever seen. From his sneakers to his cowboy hat, Clive never seemed to be lost for cash and enjoyed spending money on designer products and expensive tech gadgets without batting an eyelid.

"Cute, Daddy," Lola said giggling and lifting her arms to be held.

"Your turn, princess," Clive said, letting Lola crawl into the nursery they had made. Crawling to the blanket fort, she had built the previous night, Lola sat in the middle and watched as Clive took her orange onesie out and came to sit in her fort.

"Daddy, there's a password you have to say!" Lola said playfully trying to push him away.

"Is it, Daddy is the best?" Clive said, pulling Lola's arms through the long sleeves of the onesie.

"No," Lola laughed, standing up so Clive

could clip the three clips along her pussy shut.

"Is it, Daddy now has his little girl finally ready for bed?" Clive said, watching her. Lola shook her head, her hair flying before he pulled her onto his lap and put her hair in a messy ponytail.

"It's, Daddy, I know you took over my operation, and I'm cool with that. And also, I love you too," Lola said, kissing Clive full on the mouth, taking him by surprise. Wrapping her arms around his neck, Lola pushed her body into his, her tits rubbing against his chest and her diapered covered pussy dropping onto his cock as she relaxed facing him, her legs wrapping around his waist and resting her hands behind her, pushing herself into him.

"How did you know?" Clive said, looking at her, surprised but relieved she didn't seem to care.

"I just put two and two together. You are suddenly having all this cash, and then the bikers who had tried to take over the grocery store suddenly leaving town. Plus, I saw the paperwork that you signed for the purchase of the store. You overpaid, just saying," Lola said, smirking as she watched Clive become speechless.

"You know it's rude to go through people's private things, baby girl," Clive said, flexing his forearm and grabbing the back of her head, pulling her forward and resting her pussy against his hardening cock.

"I wasn't going through your things; I was filing. I filed that under, special secrets," Lola giggled, wrapping her arms around Clive's neck again as he rubbed her puffy, padded bottom.

"You're just as naughty as me, Daddy," Lola said as Clive stood up, Lola clinging to him like a monkey.

"Where are we going, Daddy?" Lola asked as he carried her out of the nursery.

"Well, you just told me you were a naughty girl, didn't you, sweetheart?" Clive teased, kissing Lola's cheek and the tip of her nose.

"No, I said you were naughty!" Lola giggled as Clive threw her down on his bed.

"Hmm, that's not what I heard. I heard that you were a naughty girl. And do you know what happens to naughty girls?" Clive said, tracing Lola's nipples with his fingertips until they were hard and poking through the material of her onesie.

"No, Daddy," Lola said, biting her bottom lip. Clive smirked a wicked grin as he pulled his sweats down.

"Naughty girls get fucked," he said, rolling her over, ripping open the clips of her onesie and pulling her diaper off her.

"Yeah, Daddy's naughty girl," Clive said, spanking her ass and watching as she squirmed, the diaper still between her thighs pressing against her hard clit as Clive positioned himself ready to take her from behind.

Who is Tina Moore?

Tina Moore has enjoyed the lifestyle of a Mommy Domme for several years. She began exploring kink and BDSM in her youth and found her love of being a strict Mommy Domme in early 2000. Tina Moore is now an author of many MDLG, DDLG and ABDL themed novels.

Follow her on:

Author Page on Amazon

Instagram @tinamoore.kdp

If you enjoyed this book, it would be much appreciated if you leave **a review on Amazon**.